Sins of
Blood and
Stone

John Urbancik

Sins of Blood and Stone

John Urbancik

For more information, please visit www.darkfluidity.com

ISBN: 978-1-951522-10-0

Sins of

Blood and Stone

John Urbancik

CHAPTER ONE

The gargoyle watched the woman enter St. Lazarus' Cathedral.

Her white hair, reflecting the orange tint of candle flames, fell beneath the back of her raincoat. She knelt on the maroon cushions in the front pew and bowed her head to pray.

She interlaced her fingers in prayer. Believing she was alone, silent sobs gently rocked her body.

He wanted to go to her, offer comfort, assure her that no demons walk this earth. But he didn't try to move. The shadows concealed him.

When she finally rose, the sun no longer touched the church; the moon's light failed to penetrate the thick, dark textures of the stained glass. She made the sign of the cross, whispered "Amen," and turned to leave.

Silhouettes and shadows. He knew her beauty by her liquid movements and the shape of her face, even if details escaped him.

Her eyes entranced him. He remembered a similar gaze which had contained that subtle, reined-in power.

Shadows muted her colors, but as she drew closer some details became more evident: the unobtrusive angle of nose above thick lips, the smooth skin, and moist eyes.

She was far too familiar to him. He longed to lean closer and smell the clean scent of her hair or the perfume of her body. Something inside him, something untouched for centuries, stirred.

She scrutinized him. Not even the priests ever studied him so intently. Her mouth parted, perhaps in surprise or a prelude to speech.

She crossed herself again, turned, and fled the shadows of St. Lazarus.

When she threw the doors open, an explosion of sound contaminated the church: automobiles on the street, distant sirens, the low murmur of people talking. Streetlights, only a few paces from the church, flooded the entryway, and disappeared again when the doors swung shut. The sounds remained. He had shut them out while watching the white-haired angel who had come to suffer her sins in solitude.

He didn't move to follow her, though clearly she'd seen more in him than most. He wanted to speak with her; he hadn't spoken with anyone for centuries. The demons she feared no longer existed; at least, he'd seen none more hideous than himself.

Willie Small switched off the ignition, killing the CB and Alabama tape, and climbed out of the cab of his truck. He glanced at the loading dock, where the mangy teenagers had started unloading his haul. Satisfied that he'd be stuck here almost an hour, he crossed the street and walked into the deli.

"Evening, Angie," he said, giving her his biggest smile. She wasn't much to look at, but after fourteen hours on I-95 and another two here in Manhattan, she was a very welcome sight indeed.

"Road good to you this month, Willie?" she asked. She always knew how long it had been since his last visit. He wondered if she remembered everyone this way, or if it was just because of the special tips he gave her. He even wondered how many other truckers gave her special tips, but didn't much care. Willie had to accept Angie as just another stop on the road; that's the way she wanted it.

He pulled a quart of Budweiser from the cooler, and walked to the counter. "Still pretty as ever," he lied.

"Don't bullshit me," she said, preparing his sandwich. He didn't need to tell her what he wanted, not anymore; he was as regular as they came.

"No, I'm all serious," Willie said. He glanced out the window. Granted, there were prettier girls out there. Some might have been more fun. But they cost money on these streets, and Willie wasn't into spending money when he didn't need to. And he really liked Angie, in a way he'd liked no one since his wife's death.

Angie handed him the sandwich. He savored the meat, washed it down with the cold beer. "Wish they'd send me up here more often," he told Angie.

"Yeah, yeah," she said, wiping down the table. "You know, it's closin' time."

He loved the way she spoke, with an artificial southern drawl. He smiled, and said, "Ain't it always?"

"Ain't it?" She tossed her rag across the counter; it slid and fell at Willie's feet. He picked it up while Angie locked the door. They played the same little game every time he came here, though he usually caught the rag. She took more time waddling to the door these days. He remembered a time, which didn't seem so long ago, when she'd simply walked. Before that, Willie imagined, Angie had been a young girl with a lilt in her step and something better than a deli in her dreaming mind's eye.

In the storeroom, they spent twenty minutes shoving and grunting, just as they always did. Once, someone knocked on the glass doors of the deli, screaming something about it not being ten yet, but he didn't make a nuisance of himself. The smell of sweat and road and sex helped Willie forget how much older they were now than that first time.

"You know," Willie said after they finished, "you can still come with me."

Angie laughed. "And who will feed the locals?" She meant more than just the paying customers. "Go on, get out of here. See you in another month or two."

Reluctantly, Willie walked back across the street, flipping his keys back and forth in his hand. It had started to rain while he was with Angie, but the light drizzle wouldn't keep him off the road. Four more hours, he'd be in Pennsylvania: another stop in the road where he could spend the night. Prettier than Angie, but Luanne couldn't make a roast beef sandwich any more than she could drive his rig. She wasn't anything special, like Angie. But after his wife's death, Willie had decided never to get involved that way again. Besides, Luanne had a warm bed in Pennsylvania—something Angie never offered.

The kids hadn't finished unloading his truck, but where the hell were they? At least three pallets still sat inside the back of his truck. The huge metal doors at the back of the warehouse stood open. "Hey!" he called out, tightening his fists as he walked around the storage area. No one answered.

The lights were brighter out on the loading dock than inside the warehouse, and there weren't many out there to begin with. Bare bulbs on the wall, every thirty or forty feet, lit the path well enough but left the area between pallets and boxes dark. He looked down each of those little passages, checking for the red glow of a cigarette or a joint. He couldn't think of a better reason to take a break, except to piss or eat. He saw nothing.

He reached the office, a tiny four-by-six cell with a glass partition and a flimsy, hollow door separating it from the rest of the warehouse. Better lighting: a fluorescent overhead and a lamp on the desk. A pen lay on an open, ketchup-stained accounts payable book.

"Hey!" he yelled again. Veins pounded in his forehead. He needed to get back on the road. Luanne waited for him in Penn; she expected him, and he wasn't going to be late because some fuck-ups in Manhattan wanted to go smoke a joint or catch a quick lay.

There was no loudspeaker connected to the warehouse. How the hell did they keep things running here, when even the foreman jumped post?

Willie kicked the squeaky chair and left the office.

At least two of the lights in the warehouse were out. Above him, a whole system of fluorescent lights laid dark. Did they want to go blind? Were they hiding from him? That made no sense. Playing a game? He wasn't in the mood, not while there was work to do and long hours ahead of him.

He returned to his truck. Rain fell harder now. Three forklifts sat near his truck. Two were empty, but one held a pallet from his truck. He kicked the forklift. It didn't help. He'd rather be kicking their scrawny little asses back into gear. There was no excuse for this delay.

In the corner of his eye, Willie caught movement in the back of his truck.

"You!" he said, stepping into the truck. Here, the darkness was nearly complete. If the overhead lights were on, as he'd left them, they wouldn't have broken anything. Why else would they be hiding?

The figure ahead of him straightened. Willie's eyes adjusted slowly to the dark; the kid, whoever he was, waited motionlessly.

"Where's everyone else?" Willie asked. "I gotta get out of here sometime tonight, fella. What'd you break?"

No response. Ten feet, separated only by solid darkness, the kid didn't even acknowledge him. Willie grunted a laugh; the kid was scared shitless.

Then Willie tripped on something soft and relatively small. Willie fell forward. He threw his hands out to break his fall. Sticky, wet stuff covered the floor of his truck. The smell came to him then: a sick, deathly odor, like a rat left dead behind a freezer. But it wasn't a rat; the kids hadn't spilled anything in the back of his truck but their own blood.

The figure before him loomed bigger and wider now. It spread its wings, flexed its claws, and Willie had no time to scream before seeing the huge, red eyes.

<hr />

Sitting on the foot of her bed, Neve Spirito stared out at the city. She blocked out the city sounds which penetrated her windows. The sun had fallen beyond the horizon of concrete, glass, and steel, but its light managed to filter through in a hazy, distorted way.

The city streets had never inspired fear in Neve. She knew how to avoid trouble and was strong enough to defend herself in all but the worst situations. She had nothing to fear but the ghosts in her mind. There were no ghosts in real life. The dead stayed dead, no matter how they got that way, regardless of her responsibility. She frowned, unable to convince herself. She'd seen the ghost every day for almost two weeks.

The gym provided some escape during the day, allowing uninterrupted hours on treadmills and stair climbers, or in the pool. She went to the art museums, but found it difficult to focus. Her stay-at-home vacation had turned out quite differently than expected; sacrificing days to the advertising agency felt preferable to her recent past.

She drank a lot of coffee, finding no pleasure in its taste or texture and no solace in any of the coffee shops. She went to St. Lazarus', her childhood church, hoping that maybe God could forgive her. She remembered only two prayers, the *Our Father* and *Hail Mary*, so she repeated and embellished them a thousand times. She slept sometimes during the day, but nightmares haunted her.

She'd been unable to paint since leaving the art show with Rick. The images stuck in her head: Rick giving her the gun. Rick saying, "Kill me. Stop me from sinning again." The rings on their shelves. The girl. The idea that each of those rings represented previous girls wearing those same handcuffs. The warning he'd left on her bed.

Other words haunted her as well, words repeated again tonight: "There is no justice."

The ghost stood between Neve's kitchen and living room.

Nothing in the ghost's voice or manner threatened. Still, Neve nearly forgot how to breathe. The ghostly girl wavered, flickering like a television channel which didn't come in completely. She'd been alive once, in that room.

The pallor of the woman's skin washed into her dress and white-blonde hair. She stared at Neve with melancholy blue eyes—the only color.

"What do you want from me?" Neve asked. She trembled. She knew.

The girl gave no answer, just repeated her words. "There is no justice."

Neve forced herself to inhale, but it felt sharp and sudden. The girl's image shimmered, becoming translucent and then transparent, leaving Neve alone in her apartment.

The gargoyle usually slept because of boredom. His dreams kept him connected with humanity. In his sleep, he was sometimes blessed with escape from his stone body. He was able to fly.

He never had a destination before. Tonight, he sought the woman—the angel—who had visited St. Lazarus' Cathedral.

She reminded him of his lover in too many ways, and of the evils he'd committed; hopefully, she offered him some small amount of redemption.

Thousands—millions—lived in this city. He assumed she lived nearby; why else choose St. Lazarus' when so many other churches might have been closer?

No one ever saw him, but they looked in his direction with strange, puzzled expressions. In these dream travels, no physical body burdened him and walls failed as barriers.

He found one couple making love against a kitchen countertop. Her top, torn, lay in the sink. The man pounded into her. Her limbs enveloped him like a vice, and her fingernails burrowed into his back.

They paused.

The man wiped sweat from his brow. The woman peered over her lover's shoulder, seeing only the barren white wall behind the gargoyle.

He passed through their floor, to another apartment. A man on a sofa shoved potato chips and beer into his mouth.

The man coughed and turned his head in the gargoyle's direction. He grunted, tipped the beer can over his mouth, and returned his attention to the television.

There were thousands of these apartments. The woman eluded his search. If she was, indeed, an angel sent to release him, she'd reveal herself in her own time.

His body—his prison—tugged at him. He raced back to St. Lazarus. Though a cold, stone statue waited, he feared what might happen if he resisted.

The gargoyle snapped into his body and opened his eyes.

His angel walked between the rows of pews, calmer and more confident than before. Her footsteps echoed through the cathedral.

She didn't seem to hear a second sound, like a thousand butterflies fluttering over thin, high-pitched bells. It came from everywhere. The woman, unaware, knelt before the altar to begin her silent prayers.

The sound intensified. Vaguely, the gargoyle recognized it; he'd made it himself, though he remembered little about the time between death as a man and life as a gargoyle.

A girl, an apparition, shimmered fifty feet behind his angel. No less real than the wind, she was no more substantial. "There is no justice," the ghost said.

Trembling, his angel turned. The gargoyle heard her heart's frantic pulse and her short, quick breaths. She stared, resignedly, at the ghost.

"There is no justice," the ghost repeated.

The ghost solved one mystery of the angel; it had driven her to St. Lazarus'. Perhaps she believed God might protect her.

The gargoyle remembered scattered minutes of four hundred years, all at Magdelina's grave. Ceaselessly, he'd repeated one phrase. Stuck in his throat, they'd been his last thoughts in life. He'd repeated them until, instead of waking in heaven—or hell—he woke as a gargoyle.

His angel's control amazed him. She shuddered, slightly, but did not cry. She didn't run. Every muscle tensed visibly, but she only stared at the visitor.

The ghost, in turn, did nothing.

He wanted to tell his angel she had nothing to fear. No demons hid in the darkness. Over centuries, he had seen neither demon nor devil. Only now had he been gifted with the vision of an angel.

The gargoyle moved. He sensed, rather than felt, his arm twitch. The sound of scraping stone cut the air. His heart leapt—he didn't know he had a living heart—and his stomach dropped. Instinctively, he held his breath.

But he hadn't taken a breath in over five hundred years and he had no physical heart. These overwhelming sensations struck him from memory.

His gaze never strayed from his angel as the ghost faded.

Alone, the angel stared at him. Her heartbeat echoed beneath the cavernous cathedral. She breathed more quickly but her eyes never wavered.

Never before had the gargoyle even tried to move. Now, struggling to remain perfectly still, he doubted his success. Fear, surprise, ecstasy—an onslaught of emotions he hardly recognized—caused him to tremble.

The angel looked directly into his eyes, at the life in his stone body.

She fled St. Lazarus'. The doors boomed shut behind her. The gargoyle made no move to watch her leave, didn't even turn his eyes.

Maybe this meant he could actually go to her, that he had the ability to climb from this wall and speak with his angel.

"I live," he said. The echo of his voice was deep and resonant, like gravel. These were the first words spoken in stone. The claws of his right fist flexed easily.

Had he always been able to move, or was this a gift from his angel?

Neve Spirito sprinted through the streets. The dead woman returning wasn't enough. No, something else stalked her: a creature half buried in the church walls!

And she had hoped God might help her.

The creature had been huge, a part of St. Lazarus'. It didn't need its wings, claws, or wicked teeth. Its gaze struck her. It moved. Not a trick of the shadows in the candlelight, *it moved!*

Neve ran five blocks without pausing. She dodged cars, ignored screaming horns, and knocked over maybe half a dozen people. She tried to race as quickly as her heart.

The city darkened, perhaps to match her fears.

The creature was not the ghost. It bade its time and waited for her. It was a demon, come from hell to retrieve her soul. No longer would her crime go unpunished.

She looked around to get her bearings. A short Korean man dragged down the metal fence which separated his store from the coming night. The gate made a thunderous, grating noise as it slid into place.

Neve forced herself to inhale. She forced an exhalation. If she continued breathing like this, she'd die. Behind her, dozens of faces swam in a sea of twilight; none wore a mask of stone.

A blink of red in an alley across the street caught her attention.

Neve had a side view of the alley. A creature filled those shadows. Its red eyes, fixed steadily upon her, glowed. These eyes were very unlike the statue, and unlike the ghost; these were murderous.

Neve swallowed hard, but her throat was dry. The creature flexed its claws: long, curved razors. It stood twice the size of a man. Wings extended behind it, about to burst through the buildings. Hideous teeth lined its gaping jaw. Saliva oozed over its lower lip.

It reminded her of dreams, nightmares which had receded when she woke. She'd thought they'd been about Rick, his rings, and the girl handcuffed to his bed. She'd believed the ghost had sent her images of Rick, perhaps using the knife on the girl. Did this creature, instead, haunt her sleep?

Its lips twisted into a distorted smile. From that grin, all things of nightmares invaded Neve's mind. Its voice came as a whisper in her ear. "Spirito." Her name. Nothing more.

They watched her; what gave them that right? Drawing courage from anger, she stepped closer and squinted her eyes. She wanted a better view of this third stalker. This creature's flesh was a sickly combination of green and brown. Impossibly, it seemed larger than the statue at St. Lazarus'.

Creatures hid everywhere. The demons of hell were everywhere. No matter how far or how fast she ran, they'd find her.

Apparently satisfied, it receded into the shadows and disappeared. She swallowed again.

She knew why they came. Rick. Because of what she'd failed to do. But they only frightened her; they made no threat, physically or verbally.

Neve walked slowly, newly found confidence lending her strength, back to St. Lazarus'. Where there was a House of God, a man of God could listen to her sins and offer absolution. He could tell her the prayers to make penance. She could have peace.

She watched every shadow and peeked down every alley, searching for demons. Other things existed on these streets: ribbons of darkness and garbage and winos. No demon tried to stop her.

Not long ago, she saw beauty everywhere in the world. Much of it became part of her paintings. Maybe she denied that art by taking a job she didn't need and only slightly liked, but such considerations paled in light of the phantoms. Now, she noticed the soiled aspects of life, and the dirt which no one could wash away.

Neve passed a woman pushing a stroller. The infant stared at her with the bluest eyes, as if God watched her through them. In some places, maybe the light of innocence still broke the darkness. It comforted Neve, though she had none of that light herself.

Neve threw the church doors open. This house belonged to God. No demon could wait inside. This was sanctuary. The ghost, even the statue on the wall, didn't threaten her. What, then, of the demon in the streets? Did it exist with a separate agenda?

Darkness shrouded the city. Inside St. Lazarus', candles offered some light—not unlike the baby's eyes. Neve marched down the apse.

In the wall, the statue stared at her—directly at her—like the eyes in so many paintings, but it didn't move. Its eyes were the same stony color as the rest of its body. Wings folded back behind it. Its ugly face, grotesquely disfigured, captured something of humanity.

Many statues lined the church. Gargoyles adorned the walls, inside and out. Twisted visions, many combined human features with those of cats, dogs, or other beasts. Not one moved.

The priests who served God were absent. Neve was alone.

She knelt and prayed, listening for scraping stone or the ghost's voice. Nothing interrupted.

Near midnight, she went home with a minor sense of relief, thankful for the momentary respite.

Lying in bed, Neve watched her window for signs of the creatures which haunted her world. The blank canvas on her easel stared at her, waiting for the stroke of her brush.

But she had no paintings to create. The images in her mind had transformed into ghosts and demons, nothing like the angel or the landscape which she'd displayed at the art show last week. The memories of that night, with Rick and his rings and the girl who died. Eventually, everything led Neve back to the girl, the fright in her eyes, and the momentary spark of hope which Neve had failed.

Rain poured from the morning sky by the time Neve returned to the cathedral. The storm had struck so suddenly, so unexpectedly, she thought it was directed at her. Demons stalked her beneath this cloak.

She took a deep breath, wiped her wet bangs from her eyes, and climbed St. Lazarus' steps. Thunder rumbled when she touched the door; she glanced at the gray and black sky. A shiver scraped her spine, though there was little coldness in the air.

Inside, the darkness was more complete, creating more shadows in which a demon might hide. Still, she felt safer.

In the back of her mind, Neve considered the possibility that God didn't exist, there were neither angels nor demons, and these sacred walls offered no sanctuary from whatever came with the night.

Without last night's confidence, she walked more reluctantly, trying to keep her eyes focused on Christ. The Son of God hung on the crucifix behind the altar, raised a dozen feet. Painted blood scarred his wrists, feet, and thorny crown. Neve inhaled deeply, trying to breathe the Holy Spirit in through the church's air.

Half way to the altar, she stopped and turned. Deliberately, she raised her eyes to the gargoyle.

Its twisted, snarling face gazed back at her. It was the most extravagant of the gargoyles. Others were carved into the frieze, but only a few of the other creatures were as completely formed.

What had made her think it moved? The sound—if, indeed, she had heard any sound at all—might have been the wind.

It stood poised over the center set of doors at the back of the church, directly opposite the altar. It didn't move. Its fists didn't curl and its wings didn't flap. It posed no threat. But Neve couldn't completely ignore the evidence of her senses.

Coming here might have been a mistake, but Neve was determined to follow her plan through. Slowly, she continued down the aisle. She waited, kneeling in the front pew, for her turn in the confessional.

———

"Forgive me Father, for I have sinned," she began.

Her voice sounded like an angel's should: beautiful and lilting, soft and deep. It soothed and enticed. Very much, it was Magdelina's voice.

"It's been eleven years since my last confession," she said. "I've seen things, Father, things I regret and things I fear."

Could she be descended from Magdelina? It took all his effort to keep from trembling at that possibility; there had been one daughter, five centuries ago. He remembered, too clearly, the despair on the little girl's face the day her mother died. She'd clung to him, looked up at him with sad blue eyes as though he might save her from the world. He'd failed her.

"I think, Father, I may have seen a miracle. A dark miracle, here in this church."

The priest inhaled sharply. Only the gargoyle's

accentuated hearing caught the sound.

"I didn't do anything to stop him," she continued.

Imagining his angel's lips moving as she spoke, the gargoyle saw Magdelina's mouth. "I could have stopped him. I should have called the police when it happened, at least. I ran. I did nothing. I've done nothing, and I think that's why she keeps coming back."

"Who keeps coming back?" the priest asked.

"He killed her, Father. I let him." She paused. "And now she comes back to me. To me, not to him, that's what I don't understand. She came to me yesterday, here in this church, and for the first time someone else saw her." She paused. "Maybe I've gone mad. Your gargoyle, over the doors, saw her. And I saw him."

"He watches over everything," the priest said quickly, but the pitch of his voice had risen as if a secret he'd kept had been suddenly revealed. He breathed in rapid, shallow breaths.

"There was another, too," she said, "in an alley, a couple of blocks away. It smiled at me."

"Because of the murder?" the priest asked.

She hesitated. "I think so. I'm afraid they've come to claim me, to take my soul to hell, and I hope to confess my sins before it's too late."

The priest's pause was minimal. "Your only sin, my child," he said in a rushed voice, as if he hurried to be done with the angel, "was standing by and doing nothing to save that woman. Of course she haunts your memory. You radiate goodness." He paused, perhaps to gather his thoughts. "By not acting in her defense, you've gone against your own soul. These demons, these ghosts, will only haunt you as long as you permit. The world is a beautiful place, with a minority of bad people. But when those of you who are good act, you'll find more are like you than not."

After a moment, she said, "I should have acted sooner."

"Perhaps," the priest said. He spoke more calmly, more like his usual self; the gargoyle had been here far longer than Father O'Leary's twelve years, and knew the sounds of the priest's voice. "But isn't it better to act now than not at all? These ghosts tear at your heart because you've created them for that purpose. God doesn't send ghosts to force people to do right. He trusts you, and gives you the choice to do good. He relies upon your heart and soul to guide you. He shows His belief in you every morning, with the sunrise. Every new baby is God affirming His faith in us. God is our judge, and your judge. Yet, you condemn yourself. The judge inside you says you've done something wrong, and you can still set things right, even if you can't change what happened." He paused to breathe. "That will be remembered in the next life.

"God will forgive your sins," the priest said, "but you must also forgive yourself. Go, my child, and say the Lord's Prayer. Recite the Hail Mary five times, and the Lord's Prayer again. Think, as you speak these words, on how you may heal yourself. Only when you can forgive yourself can God forgive you."

The angel said nothing more. She emerged from the confessional, walked to the front row of pews, and knelt. As she prayed, she whispered so softly that only the gargoyle, and perhaps God, heard.

She left, head bowed and silent.

After the last confession ended and the church emptied, Father O'Leary stepped cautiously from his dark booth. He looked up at the gargoyle with narrow eyes.

The gargoyle had never been seen as living before, yet the priest appeared to know, undoubtedly, that life hid beneath that stone facade.

The priest left the church through the door next to the altar. A moment later, the electric lights went out, leaving only a few dying candles.

Roxanne didn't have a regular job. She made much more money on the street, and needed every penny she got.

It was her third night this week. She hated spiked heels. She hated the tight red skirt which stopped abruptly an inch down her thighs. Her legs itched under black lace stockings.

She ignored all this, focused on the job and the benefits. Vaguely, she remembered enjoying sex. Now, it was just something she did. She reminded herself of the money, and the reason she needed it. There was no other way to earn two thousand dollars a week. She'd make more if she walked more nights, but the clientele repulsed her just a little too much.

Alleys were the worst; the idea of getting caught frightened her. A cop strolling aimlessly could stumble upon her with the john and arrest them both. They'd release the guy quickly; she'd heard of it happening to other girls.

The strip depressed Roxanne. Most of the girls here were exactly that: girls. Some were barely teenagers. These girls had mothers somewhere, worried about their little babies, not even daring to dream their girls fucked for money to pay their pimps and addictions. The girls were runaways, mostly; they never believed things could, indeed, get worse. Roxanne knew. She'd survived. Most girls didn't. They overdosed in the alleys or were found cut up and stuffed in dumpsters. Some ran away again, and though Roxanne hoped those girls who disappeared were smart enough to go home, she knew better. There were other cities, other streets, and a girl could walk them all.

Roxanne passed the newsstand. A fat guy ran the place. Leaning back on a metal folding chair and smoking a disgusting cigar, he only looked up from his perverted magazines when there was a customer or a walker. He spat comments at every girl who went by. "Nice tits," he said to Roxanne, his voice gruff and cracked. "Give daddy those things for a while, and I'll give you what I got."

She ignored him. If she looked, he'd have his hand on his cock. The poorest example of a man she'd ever seen, he sickened her. He kept the newsstand open late just so he could watch the walkers.

A black Taurus slowed alongside her. The tinted window rolled down and the driver leaned across his seat toward Roxanne.

She stopped, posing in front of the open window for a moment before leaning closer. She made sure a lot of her breasts showed. "Looking for a date?" she asked.

"Looks like I've found one," he said quickly. "How much for the whole night?"

"You think you can go that long?" Roxanne asked, a little sarcastically. She liked to issue a challenge; it made life a little more bearable knowing she could issue an unanswered challenge. She'd never met a man who could go all night, except maybe her first boyfriend. But she was fourteen, he was thirty, so boyfriend wasn't quite the right word for that.

He flashed his wallet, showing several hundred dollar bills, and smiled. She got into the car. He pulled into an alley. "Here," he said.

"All night?" It was an ugly alley. A bum slept next to the dumpster, and she heard two cats hissing and scratching at each other.

"Here," he said, getting out of the car. She climbed out. He didn't care for foreplay; he'd already stripped his pants at the front of the car. "Get this shit off," he said, grabbing her skirt in a fist. He tugged, tearing it, and Roxanne realized he was going to rape her. It had happened before. She didn't like it, but resisting was the surest way of getting killed.

"Oh, I can go all night," he said between clenched teeth. He tore her clothes off, exposing her breasts and lace panties, and threw her onto the hood of the car. It burned under her bare back; like everything else, she suffered it without complaint. She reminded herself that she needed the money for her baby, that this was just a hazard of the job. He ripped her panties off so quickly, she hardly noticed.

She closed her eyes, let him do what he would. Her body rocked with his thrusts. There was no pleasure. She knew, at least, this couldn't last all night. He'd take what he wanted and leave; if he spared her life, they'd both consider her paid. It was the price of working without a pimp. There were other, more dangerous problems than rape: the pimps who would use her, for example.

Three minutes lasted forever, but he finished. He zipped his pants and pulled Roxanne up by the hair. She swatted at his arm, instinctively.

"Bitch," he said, using her hair to fling her against the dumpster.

He was in his car before she got up. She looked down at her naked body, surprised that she was, mostly, unhurt. It could have been worse. A scar on her neck reminded her that, once, it had been a lot worse.

Behind her, the car's tires squealed as it raced away. They stopped abruptly, with a pleasing sound not unlike a drunk kicking garbage cans.

The car had crashed. She looked, hoping he'd done more damage to the car than he'd done to her.

The car's roof was caved downward, crumpled. The trunk squeezed against the brick alley wall. Blood had splashed the windshield's interior.

"Oh, God," she managed before throwing up. Nothing roused the bum; he laid in a pool of his own blood. She staggered back, retching. There was a hole in the roof of the car. Closer, Roxanne saw the man's chest, ripped open and bleeding. His head hung crookedly.

Instinct demanded that she run. She glanced at the bum again, and dismissed the thought that the two deaths were connected. She didn't know about the bum; this guy just couldn't drive.

She leaned into the car, overwhelmed by the stench. His jacket laid next to the dead body, not so heavily bloodied as the windshield and dashboard. She reached into it and withdrew his wallet.

She gathered her clothes from the alley floor. Though torn, they were something to wear. The skirt was useless, but she stepped into her panties. Her white shirt, torn down the middle, was wearable.

She flipped through the wallet as she walked to the end of the alley. *Fred Small*, the license said. She ignored the credit cards and counted seven hundred-dollar bills, four fifties, and twelve twenties: a good compensation for rape.

"Shit, girl!" The fat man at the newsstand stared as she walked down the street, cigar hanging forgotten from his open mouth. He dropped his magazine.

He looked up and down her, and the shock in his face transformed into a devious grin. "You need to come back to my place and get cleaned up, girl."

Roxanne didn't answer him, and the look of shock returned to his face. But he wasn't looking at her anymore. Something behind her. The cigar fell.

Roxanne turned around, felt the wind of something move quickly past her, but saw nothing. She spun, to face the newsstand again. The man's grin had grown, but wrongly; his throat grinned. Blood spat from his open neck, splattering Roxanne. "Oh, God." She felt the wind again, above her. She looked, but it blocked all the streetlights. She stumbled, fell to the ground. She dripped blood that wasn't her own. The creature, all wings and red eyes, replaced the sky. Roxanne whispered one last prayer: "God, protect my baby."

The wind rose. "So much like my son's mate," the creature said. Darkness dropped toward her. She saw its jagged teeth, moist with blood. She felt it touch her chest, a sharp and cold touch, and then it was gone. Its thick, putrid odor choked her.

Roxanne trembled. She laid still a long while. No one else seemed to have seen anything; there were no sirens, nobody walking near. Roxanne hugged herself, rocked back and forth on the sidewalk like a child in a cradle. She clenched her eyes shut and forced the images out of her mind.

Eventually, she left. She wouldn't get far before she was seen. Half naked, soaked with blood, carrying over a thousand dollars, she thought only of her baby, home, sleeping, waiting for what Roxanne could bring back with the money.

She ran through the street, turning down an alley to avoid eyes. She didn't want to be seen. She wanted nothing other than to get home. No more walking, never again. God, what in hell *was* that? She didn't remember what it looked like, but she remembered the wind from its wings. She knew it was huge.

She ran into someone, almost knocking him over. "My God!" he said. She didn't see him, hardly heard him, and didn't stop. She moved until she was in her tiny apartment.

The baby slept, breathing and dreaming, as did the baby sitter from across the hall. Roxanne rushed into the shower; she didn't even take the time to shut the doors or undress. She turned on the hot water and stepped in. There was blood everywhere. Someone was going to find it and follow her trail from the newsstand. No one in the world would believe her story. She didn't even know what story she could tell.

She washed, scrubbed, cried. She used soap, but everything was red. Everything. How could she provide for her baby from jail?

The water burned her skin, but she couldn't wash all the blood away. Blood from the newsstand. Blood from the car. Blood on her feet from the bum. How many others died in that alley? Why wasn't she dead?

She couldn't scrub the blood off. Or was her skin so red because of the scalding water? There was blood in her hair, under her fingernails. It coated the shower curtain, the tub, the wall. It was on the floor, and a trail led out the apartment door. She stripped what was left of her blood-saturated clothes.

The blood under her fingernails was her own, she realized. She couldn't wash it off because she'd torn her own skin in trying.

She dropped to her knees, crying, and grabbed the faucet as if it could help her. Was it, too, covered with blood, or was it just her eyes? How could there be blood everywhere? Where did it come from?

She fell on her back. Life spilled from *her*. She'd run half a mile, through oblivion, with a gaping hole in her chest. It was not the result of her scrubbing; the creature's touch had split her open!

She couldn't see straight anymore. The steam was too thick, anyhow. She didn't have the strength to stand again. Closing her eyes, she let the water scald her.

―――――――

Neve Spirito locked her door and checked all the windows. This wouldn't stop the ghost from coming in, but it gave her something to do. She couldn't concentrate on anything real. Before the night she'd met Rick, hers had been a normal life. She showered in the morning, crammed onto the subway to go work in front of a seventeen inch monitor. On days off, she visited museums, strolled aimlessly through Central Park, and hopped between bookstores and coffee shops.

But now, she couldn't even sleep or eat. Her tenuous grasp of sanity slipped slowly away.

Once, her art had come first, and then the agency—which was a type of art for her wallet, not her soul. Even this was a lie; she spent more time working at the agency than on her own art. For what? Money? Certainly, she had enough of that—her parents had left her plenty. Their ghosts never haunted her.

In the kitchen, she stared at the empty sink. In the stainless steel, she expected a reflection beside her own. There was none. In the living room, she turned on the television. Flipping up and down the channels, she found nothing which held her interest. She couldn't sit still long enough to follow an entire commercial.

It was a repeat of the night before; insomnia gripped her firmly by the throat. She paced her apartment, trying to do something, and considered walking around the block a dozen times. Again. Outside, at least, she didn't feel caged.

She should've felt safe within the familiar walls of her apartment. They were an extension of her; she knew every corner, every room, every sound and shadow. She'd lived in the apartment five years. The living room was huge, spacious, with large windows overlooking New York City. A narrow staircase led to the loft, where her bedroom-studio overlooked the rest of the apartment. Her work took every available space: paintings hung on the walls, or laid against them. Vibrant colors splattered the apartment. An easel stood unused in the corner of her bedroom. The blank canvas mocked her. Rick's letter laid on the kitchen table. It said, simply, "My Angel, I haven't forgotten you. I see you, day and night."

Angel had been the title of her painting which Rick had loved. He'd left the letter on her pillow; it had been there the night she fled him; he'd gotten into her apartment before her.

Neve was afraid to go upstairs. It was farthest from the only door out of her apartment. She didn't trust the fire escape. She felt confined, constricted.

Only two sounds remained when she turned off the television: the echo of her feet on the hardwood floors and the light rhythm of rain against the windows.

Four stories below, she saw the brake lights of cars, headlights, and people walking. Regular people, like herself. Except they lived normal lives, oblivious to the things she'd seen.

She wished she'd never visited the priest. Even confessing her sins, the details refused release. Pacing her living room, hands balled up, no solace came.

What connected the gargoyle and the creature in the alley? There were physical differences: texture and color of skin, size, the look of contempt in the demon's eyes as opposed to the serenity of the gargoyle. Did they share a purpose, in claiming her soul? Did they compete, with her as the prize? Did they battle each other now, ignoring her until one won the right to claim her? Or did they work in unison, agents of a singular destiny?

One thought was clear: they'd come for her. They'd revealed themselves to accentuate Neve's suffering in her last days.

She picked up the cordless phone. She dialed 9, and held her finger above the 1. Pressing it twice would connect to the dispatch operator, and Neve could tell everything she knew. Would confession to an authority other than God save her soul? The priest's suggestion that she forgive herself seemed sensible, but how could she make things right?

The phone's silence erupted into a wailing buzz, and she switched it off. She carried it as she paced. It comforted her; if a demon came, she had immediate access to help.

She laughed at that idea. Who could help her if a demon came? Even if someone did answer quickly enough, wouldn't they just join her in a journey to hell?

Paranoia didn't suit her. If a demon came, there was nothing she could do. Worrying about it wouldn't help her. There were no plans she could make.

"There is no justice."

The words didn't scare her anymore. The ghost paled when compared to winged teeth in an alley.

The woman stood at the bottom of the stairs, gazing at Neve. "There is no justice," she repeated.

"Justice?" Neve asked, pointing at the ghost with the phone. "There can be justice. There can be all kinds of justice." Fear and confusion frustrated her. "He can die, too. Would that be justice? I know people who can do it. I have the money." She paused. "Or do you believe in courts? Should I call the police? What in hell do you want?"

The ghost frowned.

Neve jumped back; it was the ghost's first movement. "What do you want?" Neve asked again. She trembled, unsure of her control. Everything—even the ghost—could have been her mind playing with shadows until they started moving.

"There is no justice."

"I know that," Neve said. "Do you think I can deliver justice? Or are you waiting for justice to be delivered to me?" *Was that why the demon was here?*

The ghost shimmered.

"I can't help you," Neve whispered. "He'll kill me." A second thought existed deep beneath her statement: what prevented Rick from killing her, regardless?

The ghost answered nothing.

CHAPTER TWO

At midnight, the church was empty. The candles were all extinguished, and the wind no longer pelted the stained glass windows with rain. In some ways, it reminded him of the church in which he'd served as a priest.

The gargoyle experimented.

Since hearing the sound of stone scraping stone, the gargoyle had made a conscious effort to remain still. Exposure frightened him. He knew he was too different to exist in this world. Scientists would experiment on him; priests and bishops would claim he was a servant sent down from God. Others would label him Satan's angel.

More than anything else, he feared the fact that he was different. He would not be allowed to live, not for long. He'd sent men to die for lesser differences; no man alive knew as well as the gargoyle where hysteria led. He'd been part of it, not merely a victim. Otherwise, his soul never would have come to this stone prison.

All these years, he never knew he could move. He never tried, never put the effort into lifting a finger. Now, he knew the effort would succeed. It frightened and thrilled him, and it almost overwhelmed him to just experience emotion again.

In the back of his mind, he knew he might be persecuted, hunted and destroyed as he'd punished heretics five hundred years before. This might be exactly the fate God had bestowed upon him. The gargoyle had no definite knowledge. No messenger from God came to read him his fate—which, in fact, reminded him of how he'd delivered sentences.

He wanted to move, though he might extract himself from this wall, tumble to the ground, and shatter.

He began with his hand—a talon, actually, with three claws and a thumb. It moved easily. He curled it into a fist.

He felt no pull of muscle as he moved. There was no pain, no effort. He suffered no cramps from the sudden motion after years of atrophy. There were no nerves on the ends of his finger-claws; without sensation, the body responded to his mental commands. He turned his head. He smiled.

The smile might have been grotesque. He didn't care.

He ripped his arm from the wall. A cloud of swirling dust formed, almost masking the motion. It was the dust that had gathered over a century, mixed with the dust created by scraping stone against stone. He extended his fingers, deliberately contracted his arm, and touched his cheek.

He felt nothing. He added touch to the senses lost: there was no smell, not even the taste of dust. His vision was good, but he didn't remember what it was like to see with human eyes. In the body of the gargoyle, his sense of hearing was extraordinary. He listened now to silence, and drank it in as he violated it with his symphony of stone.

He tore himself completely from the wall. Stone crumbled to dust around him, falling to the church floor. Instinctively, he spread his stone wings and glided softly to the ground. He landed between the two center columns of pews. He flexed his claws, bent his knees, and twisted his torso to see his home on the wall.

A concave hollow outlined perfectly the shape of his body—from behind. Prominent depressions showed the back of sharp talons and where his wings had folded.

He rose through the air like wind, and examined the hole. It was the perfect cast of the back of an imperfect body. His arms were grotesquely oversized, his chest wide and his legs short. Wings doubled his size.

Though solid stone, he seemed light and agile. How else would he float so freely fifteen feet above the floor?

He glided backwards, gracefully slicing the air, somersaulted and twisted to face forward, and landed at the foot of the altar.

He said no prayers. He wasn't yet ready to thank God for this freedom.

Half flying and half running, he moved to the back of the church. His legs, though short, were strong, and catapulted him down the aisle to the door. He touched the doorknob carefully with his talon; until he knew his strength, he risked destroying everything he touched. The priest already had suspicions about the gargoyle. He saw no reason to confirm Father O'Leary's ideas.

He eased the door open. New York City stared back at him; there was, thankfully, no one at St. Lazarus' steps.

The gargoyle flew over the cars and buses as he had a thousand times before in his dreams. He flew between buildings, faster than he'd ever moved in his ghostly journeys. This was no dream.

He raced faster than the cars below him. He flew over the river, under and over bridges. He passed close to the water—dangerously close, perhaps, to the boats and also the cars and the people who inhabited this world.

But he was exhilarated not to be in St. Lazarus'.

He passed over masses of people between brightly lit streets, moving too quickly to be clearly seen. Signs flashed, horns blared, the city teemed with life. No one looked up as he euphorically explored all this movement.

He turned over, flying upside down so he could look at the sky. It was only slightly visible between the concrete and steel structures which converged in the heavens.

He shot upwards. He rose over the highest buildings and into the azure sky. He passed through gloriously dark clouds. Here, the sky was black, and stars twinkled in the distance. It was as though the gargoyle had never been alive, not as a man and certainly not as a sculpture.

Could he fly to those stars? He didn't need to breathe. He felt none of gravity's pull to the earth. Was heaven above the clouds? All these years, he needed to just rise above the church and enter heaven? *Why did no one tell me?*

He continued upwards. Below, the city became a series of interconnected lights. He felt disconnected from the world. As a gargoyle, and even as a priest, he had always been disconnected, but never physically. It made him suddenly nervous.

He stopped climbing into the sky. On the ground, the sun had fallen behind the horizon, but from here he saw it low on the western sky. He wafted miles above the earth, suspended as if by thought. He wanted to reach heaven, and had no doubt that God existed. He had only to climb a little farther.

But he couldn't leave, not yet. His angel walked the city streets, pursued by a spirit. He wanted to help her, explain everything he knew about spirits to her. There couldn't be too many authorities; he'd seen no other creature who had walked as a ghost. Once condemned to repeat his last thought over and over again, the gargoyle empathized with the spirit. He knew it didn't threaten the woman.

He no longer believed she was an angel. What would an angel need with a mortal priest? An apparition couldn't frighten an angel. Therefore, he, the gargoyle, had to help her.

He began descending, aware that providing aid was a rationalization. Fair hair and skin made her strikingly beautiful. She had the walk and voice and attitude of the only woman he'd ever loved. If she was no angel, was she Magdelina returned to earth? Was she

Magdelina's child, centuries separated but still of the same blood? Did his own mortal blood flow in her veins?

———

The sun crested over the horizon. Bright reds and oranges streaked the clouds. The gargoyle landed at the steps of St. Lazarus' just as the first rays of dawn touched its highest spires. The door remained open, as he'd left it.

The gargoyle hesitated. Father O'Leary may already have entered the church. He would be standing there, staring open-mouthed at the empty spot on the wall.

He didn't want to walk in on the priest. But if he didn't return to his home, the priest wouldn't be alone in recognizing the missing statue. The risk of exposure outweighed the certainty. Soundlessly, the gargoyle stepped into the church.

Only God witnessed the gargoyle's return. He heard footsteps, though; even as the gargoyle returned, Father O'Leary approached the altar from the rectory.

Leaving the door, the gargoyle launched into the air. The door next to the altar swung open with only a wisp of sound. He twisted quickly, sliding backwards into his position. Father O'Leary stepped into the church, approached the altar, and knelt, neither looking at the gargoyle nor the back of the church.

The gargoyle slid completely into place, and winced at the sharp sound of grinding stone. Father O'Leary turned. He saw the open door, but didn't look up at the gargoyle.

The gargoyle decided to return sooner before dawn next time. Inherently, this confirmed there would be further journeys. He reveled in his newly found freedom. He wanted to soar again. More, he wanted to find his vision, the woman who resembled Magdelina so impossibly precisely. Curiosity and desire were stronger than the possibility of ascending into heaven. God had waited this long, what was another day?

Father O'Leary walked to the back of the church and pulled the door shut. Returning toward the altar, the priest stopped directly beneath the gargoyle.

The gargoyle cast his eyes down, seeing the top of Father O'Leary's head as the priest bent to examine stone dust which had fallen during the gargoyle's liberation. The priest looked up at him. Knowledge — and wisdom — hid within his old eyes. A man of God, he acknowledged miracles every day simply in breathing. Father O'Leary was a man the gargoyle might have called friend: intelligent, caring, gentle. But what would he do if he learned he shared his House with someone other than God?

Once, the gargoyle knew fear. He breathed fear. He exploited it. It was his calling. He found and bred fear, so that he might extinguish it. Yet, somewhere inside, he had always strove to be a man like Father O'Leary. Circumstances shaped him, instead, into a monster.

The gargoyle recognized the potential monster in every man, regardless of faith. When presented with something truly unknown, truly alien, the gargoyle trusted no one to react rationally. If a gargoyle lived — though not necessarily breathed — in St. Lazarus', might the priest start seeing demons every day in life? The gargoyle knew, by experience, that he could inspire a kind of passion in people, through Father O'Leary, which knew only one end: fire.

The gargoyle, of course, would be only one victim of the church's new mission. *Destroy that stone demon, cast it off our earth and back to the hell from whence it came!* The thoughts might have been overcautious, even paranoid, but better that than reckless. *And destroy all who helped bring it into existence!* The woman next, obviously a witch; how else could she have conjured such a creature out of stone? On sacred ground! The blasphemy would be unforgivable.

Father O'Leary, however, apparently saw nothing in the gargoyle to strike his interest. He returned to the altar.

The gargoyle wished for breath. He wished for flesh, for blood. He detested being a grotesque disfigurement of humanity, cursed to stand guard on Holy ground. He wanted to walk on the earth again with human feet. He would willingly surrender his wings to have arms with which to embrace his angel. So this was hell, then, to live separated from the world in which he lived.

He didn't even remember his own name when he woke, but he knew what he'd seen. He patted himself, checking pockets for whatever might exist, producing an empty flask. Its contents hadn't created what he'd seen last night.

He rolled off a rotting mattress and stumbled out from beneath the cardboard ceiling. His gold watch didn't have a big hand and the little one was stuck on the IIII. The gold was tarnished in a way real gold never did, showing signs of silver—or aluminum or something, but silver sounded better—under its top skin. He'd found it days or years ago.

He squinted under the intense sun. He scanned the big billboards and lingered on the long legs of someone whose name they wanted him to guess.

They had been around forever, but *they* couldn't prevent him from seeing last night. *They* hadn't stored him away from the night, so he'd witnessed a damned miracle. He knew it, just as well as he knew his name: *Gus*! Yes, that was his name, Gus. Gus knew what he'd seen, and he knew what he had to do.

"God is coming," he said. People stepped around him. But surely, *their* influence couldn't stretch to everyone in these streets.

9:16. He found the time, there on the billboards like he knew it would be. *They* hadn't taken everything from him if he could still find the time. He smiled, and turned to the nearest woman. She was pretty, this one, a lot like women were when he'd been young. Women these days looked more and more like young boys. He didn't like that, but there was no longer a reason to fear it. There wasn't time enough for fear.

He grabbed her by the shoulders. "God is coming."

She violently yanked herself away and shouted something nasty. He ignored her. If she didn't want to listen, she could join *them*. When God came, when God reigned over the earth, His angels would differentiate between people like Gus and people like *them*. *They* would never reach heaven, because *they* existed only to make life difficult for him.

There were others like him. He'd met some. They hid from shadows in darker corners, the only places a man could hide from the dark. The day was coming when he'd be able to walk through the streets without fear. Instead of shrugging him aside as *they* have done all these years, *they* would beg his forgiveness. *They* would beg for Gus' favor, in hopes that his favor alone might alter their fates. He had no desire to help *them*. He wished to save only those who wanted to be saved.

"Gus," an old woman said. He didn't recognize her voice or her body. Rags enveloped her, another *they* have cast out, another who would survive God's coming wrath by hiding in the dirt. "What the hell are you doing?"

"God sent His angel," Gus said. He still saw it in his mind, gliding no more than ten feet above him. "He sent His angels. It's time."

The woman shook her ugly head. "You shoulda come in las' night, Gus. You got rained on."

"God is coming," Gus told her. "He's going to save you. He's going to save me. He's going to condemn *them*. Just like it says in Revelations. He's going to condemn *them* to hell."

"C'mon," the woman said, grabbing his arm, "tell me all about it."

He let her pull him. He felt safe with her, as though they'd met before. He wasn't sure they had, but he wasn't sure they hadn't. It didn't matter, because God was coming. His stone angel had soared through the night.

***

The gargoyle closed his eyes to rest. He felt no physical exhaustion from the night before, but was weary nonetheless.

Upon closing his eyes, he immediately entered his dream travels. He floated behind the priest, who knelt in silent prayer at the altar. The gargoyle turned, to be sure he hadn't physically flown from the wall. His stone body waited for him.

In essence, he was nothing more than a spirit. Less. A spirit haunted his angel; it made itself visible, even spoke, but more restrictions limited the gargoyle outside his stone prison.

Father O'Leary rose and looked directly at him. At *him*, not his stone body. But the priest looked without seeing, for there was nothing there but the air.

The church door opened.

She stood there, silhouetted by the morning light. The gargoyle moved instantly to her, concentrating all his energy into not waking.

"Good morning," the priest called out to her.

She hesitated at the threshold. She trembled.

The gargoyle circled around and over her, drinking in her remarkable beauty: snowy hair fell almost to the small of her back. Up close, he saw, for the first time, the clear, shocking blue of her eyes. Her lips were full, the color of wine. He wanted to drink from them.

She was tall, slim, and trembling slightly. One foot remained outside the church.

He paused next to her, close enough that he might smell her perfume if his nose worked. Her hair fascinated him: pure, unadulterated white. Not the thin, stringy white of an elderly woman. Lush. Shiny. Full of energy. Reminiscent of Magdelina.

"Identical," he said. Though he spoke with no voice, the woman turned as though she heard him. She looked at him as though she saw him. Perhaps, after so many visits from the ghostly girl, she could see him.

Panicked, the gargoyle retreated to the heights of St. Lazarus'. Beneath the ceiling, far higher than his body's perch, he turned and watched the woman run out. The door swung shut behind her.

He passed through the wall of the church and floated over the woman as she walked. She hailed a taxi, glanced from side to side like she feared eyes following her, and climbed in.

He flew above the yellow car. It was a difficult task,

with so many similar machines crowding the streets. He descended into the back seat.

She stared out the window, completely unaware of the gargoyle. The driver didn't talk, except to other cars. It was a curious action, but the gargoyle had other interests. The taxi turned sharply down another road; the gargoyle continued forward a few yards before adjusting.

Eventually, the driver reached their destination.

She paid as she climbed out. Every motion was graceful, tinged by the heart of an angel. Again, she stared directly at the gargoyle. She knew he was there.

He remembered lying in the sand centuries ago. On the side of the hill, he and Magdelina had been blessed with a perfect view of the sun as it rose over the ocean. Magdelina had lain in his arms, full of trust and hope and love. They could never marry; if discovered, the Tribunal might charge him with heresy and burn him until he died.

She'd had a daughter, though never a husband. Rumors about the father never suggested the truth. She could never marry or exist in social circles where such actions—such sins—were intolerable. The people ostracized her, but she lived with it. Those were dangerous times; he couldn't leave the church and expect no punishment. Men received death sentences for lesser acts; he didn't dare risk his life for something as trivial as love.

It had been their last evening together, their last sunset. She died two days later; he and their daughter—

who never knew her father as more than priest—witnessed the execution. The charge was heresy. The trial, like all the trials, was a joke.

The gargoyle shook the memories from his head. No answers existed for his questions, not in this world.

She climbed three steps, unlocked the glass door to the apartment building, and walked in.

Soft light filled the hall, much nicer than most places the gargoyle had visited throughout his search.

She used an elevator to reach her rooms. The gargoyle rose with the machine and followed her down another hall into her apartment.

She dropped onto the couch. Unlike the other apartments he'd seen, space existed here. And color: she painted the most beautiful pictures. One caught his eye immediately: a silver cross on brown.

She breathed deeply, heavily, and closed her tearing eyes.

He moved closer, reached out to touch her. There was an energy in the air; it even touched the gargoyle, though his physical body was a stone statue standing guard over a cathedral elsewhere. His fingers—they were human fingers in this form, not those clawed talons which some sculptor had granted him—brushed against her cheek.

She jumped. He flew backwards, feeling what she felt: contact! Fleeting, momentary, their touch existed on both a physical and spiritual level. He almost passed through the walls, afraid to be seen, but it was too late for that.

"How many of you are there?" she asked. She looked through him; invisible, he doubted he was intangible. *She had felt his touch!*

The gargoyle saw only one explanation: the energy which made up their souls had connected. Somehow, whether by blood or by the fact that in another life, another time, she was his lover, it was inescapable.

It frightened him; she, too, was frightened. She looked from side to side, paranoid now, afraid there were demons and devils in every shadow.

But I am no devil, no demon! he wanted to scream. *I have seen no demons in all my years, and I have as many centuries as a man might have decades!*

She heard something of his silent scream. No words, but she responded to the intensity. She looked at him again, directly where he floated. "What do you want with me?" she asked. Her body trembled. He didn't want to inspire fear in her, he wanted to quell it! Failing yet again, he fled.

He tried to think, tried to figure out what went wrong. There was no way to know, not without speaking with the woman. But wasn't that exactly what he wanted to do?

He couldn't. She was scared enough as it was; a ghost haunted her. She thought demons had come to claim her for hell.

He opened his eyes, instantly back at St. Lazarus'. Father O'Leary still knelt before the altar. The gargoyle wondered how the priest had reacted when the woman opened the door and then left. Had he recognized her as the haunted confessor? Did he try to run after her, to console and comfort her? The gargoyle knew only that he had tried exactly that, with exactly the opposite results.

Frustration tightened his fists. He ignored the stony sound which echoed beneath St. Lazarus' ceiling. The priest turned, watched the wall and even looked at him, but the gargoyle no longer cared. He was angry with himself; his curiosity had thrown his angel further into the depths of her personal abyss.

The woman was identical in every way to Magdelina: her voice, the curve of her hips, the sound her breath, her thick lips and petite nose. There was no reason to believe they were the same women. There was, however, no reason to believe they were not. Why, after all these years, would Magdelina come to him now? He questioned his belief in heaven and hell, and more specifically in God and His angels.

After years of watching and listening and nothing else, the gargoyle was miraculously able to move? If God existed, wouldn't He release the gargoyle from the confines of St. Lazarus' Cathedral to seek out and destroy this demon which stalked his angel? Was that what he must do to earn ascension into heaven? Was this proof of God?

The woman had no answers; she sought them. There was only one person to whom he might turn for advice.

The church was empty. The gargoyle hadn't heard Father O'Leary leave. The priest knew something about him, or at least guessed at the truth; what harm could there be in confessing his sins to a man of God?

"Forgive me Father," he whispered—his voice surprisingly deep and strong, far smoother than he would have imagined in a voice escaping the bowels of a statue—"for I have sinned."

He waited. After so many years of doing nothing else, mere minutes now lasted an eternity. He had nothing external to judge the passing of time; there were sounds from the street, muffled through the great walls of the church. Daylight filtered through the stained glass windows and never changed gradually; when evening fell, daylight abruptly ceased to enter. Because of the light that came into the church, he knew the day had not ended.

Over and over again, for a hundred years, he had reviewed his sins. He'd relived every minute of his life, good and bad, and knew his mistakes in retrospect; the past was unalterable. Until his angel came to the church, he'd had nothing to do but remember. The future was as uncontrollable as his past.

The woman, she'd inspired these thoughts into frenzy. He hated his most vivid memories. He didn't like watching the woman he loved burn to death in a public execution. He didn't like to look down into their daughter's wide blue eyes and see moisture gathered inside them.

Not once had he confessed these sins. Repentance? Was that what was required before he could ascend into heaven? Even if he didn't reach heaven, his existence would be far more tolerable if his mind escaped the past. By putting his actions into words, by releasing the demons haunting his head, could he free himself of their burden?

He waited for Father O'Leary to return. He wanted to tell someone what he'd done. He wanted to tell the woman, but she had enough problems already. To help her, he needed another method to release his burden. He had to confess his sins, and place himself at God's mercy.

The priest approached the altar from the side door. The gargoyle recognized Father O'Leary's footsteps and rhythmic breathing.

Father O'Leary eyed him a moment, and then, silently, knelt at the altar. He crossed himself and began to pray. The gargoyle slid from his place in the wall, and extended his wings. He knew he must be cautious; if the priest was too afraid, how could he hear a confession? How could he offer absolution?

"Father O'Leary," he said, softly, "will you hear my sins?"

The priest, trembling visibly, didn't turn from the altar. "Of course," he said. His voice raised slightly in pitch. "Actually, I've been expecting you."

The gargoyle landed beside the priest. Father O'Leary turned slowly. There was something of fear in the priest's eyes, and something of awe, but he fell victim to neither. Instead, he turned back to the altar and completed his prayer. He then rose and walked to the confessional. He pulled back the curtain for the gargoyle.

The gargoyle retracted his wings; they become almost a part of him, an extension of his back. He stood two feet taller than the priest, and was at least twice as wide, but the gargoyle fit into the large confessional booth.

A moment later, Father O'Leary slid the partition open.

The gargoyle crossed himself, concluding with "Amen." He was nervous; he'd never told this story. No one alive, no one dead, no one but God knew the things he was about to say. "*Ignascere maiores ob pecavi,*" he said. "It has been five hundred years since I last received Reconciliation.

"There was a time when I had a name, but my name no longer matters. I am merely a gargoyle now, a decoration condemned to defend this church against demons which never come. During my life, I committed the most mortal of sins. Some, I did out of my faith, my belief." He paused.

CHAPTER THREE

"I was born in the Year of Our Lord 1469, in a small town a hundred miles or more from Madrid. I was ordained seventeen years later and served Our Lord faithfully until the summer of my twenty-first year. It was then that I met Magdelina."

She'd been young; her parents had brought her to be punished for the blood which passed between her legs, but the gargoyle mentioned none of this.

"Of the devil," her mother had insisted, thrusting the girl at him. Magdelina, shy and innocent, cast her moist eyes down. She'd appeared as an angel, with a soft halo of white hair around her head. "Keep her," the mother had said, "until she learns."

But what could a priest teach her?

She, instead, over the next few months, taught him how to kiss. The taste of her mouth lingered even now. She'd woven the most beautiful stories, and elegantly intertwined physical contact into those tales.

When Magdelina's parents fell to plague, she'd still been in the church's care. After they died, she'd moved into her parents' tiny home.

The gargoyle told none of this. "For the first time, I questioned my devotion to God. I considered risking excommunication to marry this woman; she'd stolen from me my heart, my desire, my reason to breathe. An hour did not pass when she did not enter my mind. She was beautiful, fair, unlike most women in the area, her hair pure white. Not brittle like an old woman's, but soft. And long. God had gifted her with the most amazing shade of blue in her eyes. Even the sky, which I saw again only this morning, paled in comparison. She was quiet, almost pliant. She confessed her sins to me, and made up stories.

"I may have acted out of love, but I know little about that word. What is love, if it can alter the heart of a Holy Man? What is love, if it can turn a man against the very core of what he believed? And still, I say that love drove me in those days.

"We shared wine, food, song; it was a good time for some, but less fortunate for most. Queen Isabella had just petitioned the Pope, successfully, for an Inquisition to root out heretics. I thought it fortunate when I was chosen to lead The Inquisition in my hometown." The gargoyle paused a moment; he didn't listen for the priest's responses, either verbal or simply in breath or the sound of shifting in his booth. The vivid memories, rich and full of blood and life, blocked out everything external.

"I thought this was good for me," he continued. "It renewed my faith, this divine mission. I sought out heresy without mercy. The courts I set up to prove guilt were simple and ridiculous: the accuser presented his evidence, and from this I judged. I, and I alone, judged the fate of every man, woman, and child brought before me under the authority of the Tribunal.

"One man, whose name I don't remember, was accused by his neighbor. 'I've seen him in his best suit,' the accuser told me, 'on the Hebrew Sabbath. He fails to recognize Christ as his savior, and continues to worship in his mother's faith in private while attending our church, your church, in clothing which is less than his best.'

"I considered this evidence, ignoring the fact that the accuser would win disputed land if his charges were found justified. His argument convinced me that the accused did indeed celebrate God, but he didn't accept Jesus Christ as The Lord, Our Savior. He didn't accept Jesus Christ as the Son of God. Based on the words of this man, without even examining the clothing in question or listening to anyone else, I ordered that the accused either confess and repent, and beg God's forgiveness—at which time I might reconsider the claim against him—or be burned to death. I gave him three months to prepare his confession.

"In those three months, he insisted that he'd done nothing wrong. The guards chained him to the wall, denied him food and drink—except the bare minimum to live—and ate their own meals upon a table five yards from him. 'You may eat,' the guards told him, 'when you confess.'

"'I have nothing to confess!' the man cried. He prayed, chained to that wall. He recited the Lord's prayer continually. He cried, he screamed, he begged for water. He thrashed about in his chains, drawing blood from his wrists and ankles. He offered bribes to the guards, but they were good Christian soldiers and would not be swayed by a heretic's ravings. They informed me of his three months in captivity, told me the man had refused to confess or accept Jesus.

"I took all this on faith. I took this from their mouths, accepted it, and ordered the man's execution.

"Execution by The Inquisition came primarily in one form. The condemned was tied to a stake and burnt alive. I witnessed every execution I ordered. This man screamed, like all the others. He begged for me to put out the flames before they engulfed him, until he could no longer speak coherently. I won't describe to you the effects of fire on the human body. Let me just say, it was not a pleasurable experience, even for witnesses."

Not describing the details didn't keep them from the gargoyle's mind. The scent of burning flesh overwhelmed his memory, and the sound of twigs—or bones—cracking as the flames consumed the heretics echoed in his mind.

"A year after our affair began, Magdelina gave birth to a girl. The town labeled her a tramp. It was a crime she'd committed, and a sin. She came to church daily to see me, even if only to watch me perform mass, and the townspeople believed she sought forgiveness from God. Still, they shunned her, accusing her of sleeping in the beds of every man. Women became angry with their husbands if Magdelina glanced at them, even if the look was peripheral, momentary, or accidental. No one accused her of heresy; mostly because no one had anything material to gain from her condemnation.

"They assumed I knew the child's father—and in fact, I did—but no one asked me. I'd earned a reputation: tough, faithful to God, relentless in my pursuit of pagans and heresies. No one survived, once charged, under my rule. If they confessed, they were burned alive for their actions. If they didn't admit to their crimes, they were burned for their lack of repentance. Many died in prison before we had a chance to execute them.

"I took pleasure from what I did. I believed it was for the good of God, for the good of the Church. I acted under direct orders from Queen Isabella and Thomas of Torquemada, and in the best interest of my Lord. I truly believed I worked His will.

"But I didn't always act in the best interest of God, or even myself. In four years, I put 462 people to death. In September of 1498, everything that was my life changed. Only three more people would die because of me."

The gargoyle paused. He knew, now, that his pursuits had been more fueled by hysteria than anything else. He'd accepted his excuses when he was young, hadn't considered the consequences of his actions. He made a lot of money for the church, through confiscation of land and property. He followed blindly what he was told, and killed a lot of men whose worst crime had been wearing a good suit on the wrong day of the week.

He'd had centuries to consider what he'd done, and he had never been able to reconcile with himself. No Act of Contrition could erase the sins he'd already confessed to Father O'Leary, but he hadn't told the priest anything yet. Still, he continued.

"In the middle of that September, I did far worse than I could ever have imagined possible."

⸻

Neve Spirito reached the church and halted at the door. To the left and right, people walked and cars scampered about. Everything felt distant. She hadn't been part of this world since the ghost first spoke to her. Her world had become one where shadows hid demons, where the watchful eyes glowed an iridescent crimson. The color of fire and hell. The color of blood.

She'd dreamt of Christ. Nailed to the cross, he whispered something about salvation. This morning, she felt eyes upon her where there were no mortal eyes. The church may offer sanctuary, but no one guaranteed it. There were only the priest, a simple man living a simple life, and the stone gargoyle which hung above the door.

She remembered how the gargoyle had apparently moved in the flickering light of the candles. Was she so afraid of the gargoyle that she couldn't enter the church?

She touched the door. It was still early. She didn't expect the priest to recognize her from earlier, though he might remember her confession. She'd failed to provide him with details, but he hadn't believed her story anyhow. He thought she simply imagined the ghost, that something inside her had created the image which haunted her. He thought the ghost and demon were a part of her conscience, pushing her to do right and bring about justice which the ghost insisted didn't exist. For someone who put his faith in a God he neither saw nor spoke with, he put an awfully small amount of faith in her experience.

She wouldn't have believed the story any more than he had. She might have suggested, in fact, that the person seeing ghosts visit a psychiatrist next. What had she expected him to do?

She expected nothing. She wanted to pray, in solitude, before the altar. She wanted to beg God for mercy. She wanted to wipe the whole world from her mind, both the real and supernatural worlds, and start fresh when she emerged. She wanted to find a solution which wouldn't kill her. No priest could tell her what words to say. But this was God's home, which she and her parents had attended every Sunday for much of her earliest years, and somehow praying here added the strength of her parents' beliefs to her own. No other place on earth offered absolution.

She crossed herself, shoved the door open, and strode in.

The church appeared larger, emptier; there was no one at the altar or in the pews. The door swung shut behind her, locking out the sounds of the real world, permitting her to dive completely into this one.

Half way up the aisle, Neve realized she wasn't alone; there was a voice, muffled and deep. It originated somewhere ahead of her, off to the side: the confession booths. She stopped and listened.

"In September of 1498, everything that was my life changed. Only three more people would die because of me. In the middle of that September, I did far worse than I could ever have imagined possible."

1498? The priest dealt with crazier people than she'd imagined.

She looked around, to be certain she was alone. This confession interested her. It surprised her, that she heard the man speak; she'd thought confessionals were sound-proofed.

The pews were empty. The door on the side of the altar was shut tight. Even the gargoyle, standing above the door, was absent.

She grabbed the pew next to her to keep from falling. The gargoyle that had watched her, which she'd heard move, had vanished. There was a depression in the wall where it had been, as if someone had carved the back of a gargoyle into the wall rather than the face out of stone. The statue really had moved!

Slowly, very slowly, she turned her head to the confessional. The doors were shut so she couldn't see inside. She couldn't help but wonder: was it the gargoyle's confession she overheard?

<hr />

The gargoyle paused. Images swirled through his head. Instead of freeing him of the burden, the telling brought him closer. He felt, speaking to the priest, the same rock in his gut which had plagued him that September morning. He'd had centuries to think about what he'd done. He'd seen men come and go from St. Lazarus' with the same vehement beliefs: to purge the Christian world of all that was evil, of all that was of the devil. It didn't take the gargoyle all this time to realize that different opinions were not cause enough for death. Despite the fundamental differences between the ideology of the Catholic Church and the hundreds of heretics he'd put to death, their basic belief systems were the same: there was a God, creator of all things upon heaven and earth. Heaven waited after life had passed, and everyone had a soul which strove for, but fell short of, perfection. The pagans and heretics only had different names and mythologies around their respective gods.

Five hundred years after burning so many different thinkers and accused dissidents, regardless of the weight—or lack thereof—of the argument against them, the gargoyle couldn't justify his own actions.

And the worst, of course, was Magdelina.

"I awoke one September morning to find one of the townsmen standing at the foot of my bed," the gargoyle continued. "He startled and upset me. I recognized his face but didn't know his name, and immediately demanded an explanation.

"'I know what you've done, *Father*,' the man said to me. He spit the last word out, as though I deserved no title. I didn't realize, then, how right he was. I knew exactly what he meant, though; he had seen Magdelina and myself together. He'd seen us in the act of love, the same act which created our daughter. He knew this, and knew, also, that I was a father in more than one meaning of the word.

"I didn't know how he knew. I didn't care. I rose from my bed and struck him. He went down without a fight. It surprised me, that I was able to do this; all my life, I'd been devoted to God. Never had I fought with a man before, and here my first altercation ended before it had even begun.

"When he opened his eyes, he did so to darkness. I had him taken to the deepest of the dungeons. I personally bound him to the wall and sealed the underground chamber. I left him there. I gave him no food, water, or even light. Not even the rats could get into his chamber. Three days later, after I'd decided my course of action, I went down to the sealed chamber. 'Do you confess?' I asked the wall. I spoke barely above a whisper; maybe I feared he might gain supernatural strength in his imprisonment. A part of me knew that what I was doing, what I was planning, was wrong. I'd locked him there without anyone even suggesting heresy.

"No one questioned his disappearance. I never bothered to learn his name. Many people disappeared in those days, and it was generally assumed that they stood before the church to answer for their crimes against God.

"After my whispers, he screamed. His cries were incoherent, his voice raw. I don't think there were many words in what he said. He cursed me; I know he wanted me damned to hell. I realized, then, that I would stand before God and have two sins to confess: the woman, and his murder. The other executions didn't concern me. My conscience, until that day, had been clear. But no longer. My course of action was set.

"I couldn't risk freeing him. His return would have signaled my weakness. Being feared had its advantages, and I took them often—things in which I saw nothing wrong. More than that, though, I couldn't have him tell others what he'd seen. I never considered that his accusation might not have involved Magdelina. The possibility frightened me; his may have been a separate accusation.

"I had other lovers. I didn't know a man alive without at least one. From my position, I could afford several. I did, however, know the difference between visiting a common whore and fathering a child—the only fatherless child in the region. How would people react if they learned the truth? In this, I was afraid. It was an unrealistic fear, for what could they have done? I was afraid for my love for Magdelina, not for our indiscretion. Still, I needed to be sure it never happened, and I thought there might only be one way. I had to never see Magdelina again.

"Which, of course, was impossible.

"For three days, I thought about it," the gargoyle continued. He didn't mention the five hundred years afterwards. "I believed that I must never see Magdelina again. I cried about this, but I foolishly convinced myself I had enough strength to carry out my decision." He lowered his voice. "If I had truly been strong, I would have resisted this decision.

The gargoyle paused, glad only that his stone eyes could shed no tears. "She had to leave. I wanted to send her to another town. I had an uncle some three days travel away, I could arrange for her to stay there. But the risk remained. What if she came back? What if I went there? No, I decided the only way to solve my problem—a problem which existed solely in my mind, remember—was if one of us died. As long as we both lived, I would seek out her touch, I would long for her embrace and kisses. There were other kisses to be had in her absence; but knowing she lived, other lips would taste pale. Because I truly loved her. I knew that then, as surely as I know it now. I just lied to myself. I thought that if Magdelina left, these emotions would follow. Remember, not a day went by, then or since, when I didn't think of her. I don't wish, now, to reconcile with God so much as I need to reconcile with her.

"I charged her with heresy. Soldiers took her in the middle of the night, and I went shortly afterwards to retrieve our daughter.

"'What happened to mommy?' she asked me. She cried. She knew only that darkly dressed men had come and forcibly taken Magdelina. Her blood stained the floors.

"I lied to the child—my child. She was only a few years old—seven, maybe. I told her the evil men meant to burn Magdelina alive, that I could do nothing to stop them. I promised to punish those responsible. In a way, I fulfilled this promise.

"I tried Magdelina in silence, convicted her based on evidence I alone conjured. No one defended her; many who had tried to help accused heretics had suffered the same fate, guilty by association. I excluded our daughter from the trial. I took the girl into my home, cared for her, showed the townspeople I was not a heartless beast. I fed her, bought her good clothes, made sure she would have the best teachers.

"But I took her with me to the burning. In bed the night before, I hid my tears from the world, but not from God.

"Almost a month had passed since my soldiers took Magdelina; she'd been raped, beaten, completely devastated in prison, but I never went to comfort or console her. The guards told me, once, she'd requested an audience. They didn't said she begged to see me, but I imagined she did. I would have. No one else could have been responsible, and surely she suspected she'd done something wrong. But she hadn't. The reason was far simpler than that: I was weak."

He paused. He hated the images in his minds: fire consuming his lover and beloved. Magdelina had struggled silently. Her hands bled as she tried to free herself. Moisture, unshed tears, stained her eyes. She'd been strong. He'd failed her. He'd failed himself.

The memories threatened to stop him. But he was almost done. If there was any redemption to be had, the gargoyle at least needed to tell the facts. The images clung to his mind, though. Magdelina's face intertwined with the face of his angel. Would he fail her, too?

"Our daughter clung to my leg as the fire consumed her mother. Magdelina did not scream even once. I told our daughter not to look. I told her not to listen. Too late, I realized how cruel it had been to bring her.

"The girl had inherited her mother's brilliant features: the long, pure white hair; exquisite blue eyes; a tall, slim body. She was but a child, seven or eight, and I saw so much of her mother in her. Nothing of me. Nothing of the monster I'd become. When she looked at me, something contaminated the sadness in her eyes, a sense of wisdom or knowledge. She knew, in that moment, that her mother's death was my responsibility. I saw then, in this girl's eyes: I no longer worked for the good of God.

"The following day, I executed the last heretic of my career." He clenched his eyes shut, holding back tears which could not flow.

The gargoyle paused in his story. He'd left out details, either to spare Father O'Leary or himself. If the latter was his reason, he failed; images flooded his mind.

He went, once, to see Magdelina before her execution. She never knew he came. Hidden safely in the shadows, he watched. She laid there, on the cold stone floor, in the tattered ruins of her dress. The blood had never been cleaned from her and was now a crusty red above her eye, across her cheek, and down the side of her arm. A single, distant candle kept her company.

He'd heard how savagely she had resisted the soldiers, how she'd spilled more than a little of their blood. By the time he came to watch her, they had beaten the fight out of her. It was impossible, in the shroud of the dungeon, to differentiate between the blood and dirt which stained her tattered dress.

There were whispered tales that she was a witch, beguiling men at will; this story served the town well, freeing women to forgive their husbands. He knew Magdelina wasn't pure; she'd taught him much during their time together. She was the adventurer, the aggressor. She mastered the moment, writhing and moaning all about him. And never was their passion the same. Her variations led him to believe whole religions might be devoted entirely to sex. It comforted him to consider Magdelina a heretic, practicing some magical art of the flesh. She'd woven her spells around him quite nicely. Perhaps when she died, the attraction—the love, but at the time he refused even to think of the word—would die away.

A rat crawled across her leg. She neither cringed nor screamed. She barely looked at it, turning her eyes but not her head. When the rat scurried off, Magdelina drew her leg closer to her body.

She'd always been beautiful. All women were beautiful, he reminded himself, but some more than others, and few like Magdelina. When she smiled, her thick, savory lips parted slightly, and his need for her burned like fires in hell.

"Almost a full day passed after that," the gargoyle continued. "I locked myself in church, allowed no visitors and none of my congregation to enter. I mourned in my own way, crying before the altar, begging God for forgiveness, for a sign that I wasn't as evil as I believed.

"In killing Magdelina, I'd sacrificed my soul to the devil. I displaced myself as one of God's chosen. No longer was I fit to wear the robes of a priest. No longer was I fit to seek out and expose the heresies around me.

"In the middle of the night, I went to the pyre. Smoke still rose from the embers, and I burned myself twice as I gathered Magdelina's ashes. I collected her remains in the golden grail of my church, and went to the river. I dug a hole, with my hands, and buried the grail. I prayed for her happiness in heaven, went through the motions of last rites though I doubted I could give them anymore.

"I returned to the church and prayed. No one came to bother me. Near midnight, I gave up my prayers. There was no absolution. In trying to protect my physical life, I'd destroyed any chance of a spiritual one. That's part of the reason I'm here, in this statue, today.

"Having given up, I took my life there in the church. I ran myself through the blade of a sword. Blood poured out beneath me, and I knelt before the statue of Christ for as long as I was able. He stared at me no differently than ever. The candlelight played no tricks with my mind, and the onset of death didn't alter my perceptions. Despite all my wanting and wishing and praying, the statue of Christ refused to move. He didn't smile upon me, didn't put His hand out to me. He offered no salvation, no solace, no sympathy. He allowed me to die, and for that I hated Him. I hated Jesus and I hated God for what He allowed me to become. I hated myself more.

"I don't know what happened to my body. Blood streamed out of me. Strength faded to the point that I could hardly lift my head, so I closed my eyes. Next, I stood at the riverside grave of my beloved Magdelina. Alone, I stared down at it. Some time had passed, though I couldn't say how much; fresh grass grew over the mound of earth, but it clearly had been recently made. I said, 'I loved you, Magdelina.'

"I was incapable of anything more. I couldn't move; that grave was, essentially, my haunt. I was there sometimes, and at other times I was nowhere at all. I have no memory of those times; I saw neither heaven nor hell. And not once did someone happen upon me as I told Magdelina I loved her.

"I had no way to judge the passing of time; sometimes it was day, sometimes it was night, and after what seemed to me a very short time, there was nothing to differentiate Magdelina's grave from the earth around it. Time wiped it from the earth, and apparently wiped me away, too.

"I never visited my own grave. I don't even know if I had one. I never saw the church again. All sensations had ceased with death.

"I still feel no pain, no cold or heat, nothing through my stone skin. I can't feel my own hands if I hold them together.

"I believe it was 1878 when I opened my eyes in St. Lazarus' Cathedral. I didn't know how old this church was, but I recognized the stone prison my soul came to rest in. I knew then what my punishment must be: stand and guard the House of God from demons, as gargoyles do.

"But demons never came. I've been here, unmoving, over a century, and only recently did I learn I could move or speak."

The gargoyle paused. He had confessed his sin. Should he continue his story?

The priest answered his question. "How did you learn that you could, in fact, move and speak?"

Neve Spirito listened to the priest and confessor. She didn't know how she heard them, when they didn't seem to hear her. Maybe their voices carried more when the church was empty. But then, wouldn't her footsteps have echoed as loudly, and the sound of the door when she'd opened and closed it?

"How did you learn that you could, in fact, move and speak?" the priest asked.

Neve knew the answer. She'd been coming to this church, to pray in solitude, every evening since the ghost first appeared. Neve was exactly as the gargoyle had described the girl: tall and slim, long white hair and crystalline eyes. She trembled, wondering if she was Magdelina reborn, or a descendant of Magdelina and the gargoyle. She felt no fear; the gargoyle, despite her initial reaction, admitted that he was here to protect her from demons. He alone could vanquish the red-eyed creature which had watched her from the alley, and perhaps the ghost as well.

"I don't know exactly when it started," the gargoyle said. "I became aware of her gradually; I don't know her name, but I now know where she lives. I have left things out, Father, like my dreams. I visited her in a dream today, and frightened her when I meant to reassure. Part of my punishment, I'm sure.

"Physically, she is Magdelina. She is our daughter. I moved, I believe, to find out who she was, what she really was. I hope she is Magdelina, returned to earth in angelic form to release me from this prison. I don't need God's forgiveness as much as I need hers. If this woman is an angel, she can release me and I can then either ascend into heaven or descend into hell. But I know no way to approach her."

"I'm no angel," Neve said under her breath. She held responsibility for the girl's death.

"Father, I have prayed for more years than you've been alive. I have asked God's forgiveness. I've asked for a divine sign. I've been given nothing, so in my final attempt at reconciliation with God and Magdelina and myself, I've confessed these sins to you."

Neve wiped a fledgling tear from the corner of her eye. Fear struck her. The confession was nearly over. When they emerged from their booths, they'd find her listening. Though in her head she believed the gargoyle wasn't here to claim her for hell, her racing heart disagreed.

She turned swiftly, conscious of every sound. She felt like a peeping Tom. Heat rushed to her face. Neve hurried out of the pew, and in her hurry banged her leg against the hard wood. Pain echoed throughout her leg, and sound throughout St. Lazarus'.

⚓

The sound brought the gargoyle's confession to a premature end. He had nothing more to tell, but the priest hadn't delivered Penance yet.

The crack of a leg against wood was followed by a quick, tight inhalation of breath. No longer wrapped up in his own story, the gargoyle heard the sounds of the church: a slight breeze blowing against the rich stained glass windows, footsteps, and erratic breathing.

His angel. She'd heard. He didn't know how much, but he recognized the sound of her breath.

He emerged from the confessional and saw his angel running down the center aisle. She reached the heavy front doors, threw one open, and glanced over her shoulder.

Light fell in around her, casting her in silhouette as the painted image of divinity. White hair twirled behind her as she turned, catching beams of sunlight. City sounds exploded from beyond the open door. Even from the confessional, the gargoyle saw how many people filled the street.

She stepped out, and the door closed behind her.

Father O'Leary stood next to the gargoyle. "A ghost haunts her."

"I know."

⌐⟶⌐

Neve Spirito escaped the church and threw herself, breathlessly, into the first cab she found. She had looked back before leaving St. Lazarus', confirming suspicions, hopes, and fears. The church doors didn't open as the taxi pulled away. The gargoyle did not chase her.

She didn't expect him to chase her. She'd heard his story, or part of it, which suggested that he hadn't come to take her soul. The other things were another question.

She shouldn't have run. She'd done absolutely nothing wrong; the gargoyle had spoken loudly enough to be heard, perhaps because he wanted—needed—her to hear. How else could the gargoyle approach Neve?

The taxi swam through the streets. She didn't remember telling the cabbie where to take her, but didn't care as long as it was someplace else.

The driver stopped somewhere alongside Central Park. She paid him and walked down the trail. Bicyclists and skaters zipped around her. With people around, she thought she'd be spared from the ghost. The demon might hide in the trees, but maybe daylight provided safety. It had been the last light of twilight in which she'd seen it before.

"You!" a man cried. An ugly man, a bum wrapped in too much clothing for this warm weather, pointed at Neve. A crazed look glazed his eyes, and an equally ugly woman tried to hold him back.

"You!" he said again, stepping closer. Neve increased her pace. "God is coming," he called after her. "God has sent an army of stone angels to our earth. He can save you, or cast you out with them."

Neve wanted to ignore him, but his angels were stone.

"God comes for all of us," he said, following as Neve slowed. "Put your faith in God. All things will work out. He's returned to put us in our rightful place."

Neve studied the man for a moment. Almost a foot shorter than Neve, uncontrolled gray hair and dull blue eyes scarred his face. There was only enough strength in his hands to clutch the brown paper bag which held a bottle. He reeked of alcohol. He stared steadily at her; the only power at his command came through in the intensity of his eyes. "You are one, I can tell," he said.

"I'm not an angel," she told him.

His smile broadened. "And I'm no saint," he said, swinging his arms, "but we shall be saved! He has come, His angels have come in bodies of stone to vanquish The Grand Adversary and his minions from this earth of ours forever. Eden will exist here, when they are gone. You and I shall be a part of that."

The woman behind him tried to pull him back again; though older and shorter, she appeared stronger. Her eyes reflected actual life, not the man's dull comprehension of a spirituality he couldn't understand. She kept her short white hair neat, and had carefully arranged her tattered clothes.

"Lay your hands off me, woman!" the man screamed. He pulled away from her and looked frantically about. "You say you want to be with me, but in truth you want me to be with you. Always, you lead, and I follow. I don't even know your name, woman!"

"You're causing a scene," she said.

The scene played only for Neve's eyes; the park seemed suddenly empty. "Unhand me!" the man cried.

"I'm your wife, Gus," the woman said, "not just some woman you met on the street." He quieted, but didn't quite surrender. "Now, you come with me, or there won't be any second coming for you. Hit on another young girlie, and you won't live that long."

He drew a deep breath, and turned to Neve. "We'll meet again, you and I. You'll see." He turned to his wife. "You'll see also, woman."

"I'm sure I will," she said.

⚓

The gargoyle returned to his perch and waited for the day to end. Under cover of darkness, he planned to return to the woman's apartment. He didn't know what she heard, and didn't care; he wanted her to know everything. Neither angel nor devil, his was a soul that continued to pay for his mistakes. He wanted to blame the hysteria of the time, the general consciousness, but knew the choices had been his. He could have judged someone, even one person, innocent. Perhaps it would have changed things if he'd decided that not only was that person innocent, but their accuser instead must face death—only a heretic, he could have explained, would falsely accuse another. That might have quelled the hysteria. But decisions to change the past resulted only in frustration.

He wanted to tell his angel how little control he had as a spirit: he returned to the grave, cried and said *I loved you, Magdelina.* Nothing else. He couldn't touch a flower or smell the moisture in the air. He heard the river, but felt no coldness when winter came. He saw the grave, but couldn't turn his head to look behind him. The ghost haunting her now, surely, could do little more, though this spirit returned to a person.

Father O'Leary knelt before the altar, praying. The gargoyle wondered what thoughts went through the man's head. There were other people in the church now; the gargoyle had been blessed with privacy for his long penance. The day had only just begun; life teemed outside the big doors below him. Too anxious to rest, he didn't know if he could remain still for the hours which remained in the day. Centuries, he'd managed without difficulty. Yet every minute that passed now was one more minute in which the woman could arrive at the wrong conclusion, another minute in which his angel's fear might grow.

She might return to St. Lazarus'. He hoped she would. He hoped that she'd come to an empty church, so he could speak with her as he'd spoken with the priest.

He reviewed the methods of exorcism. No one had ever asked him to perform one; no demons had haunted his town. He'd studied the method once, in preparation, and over five hundred years later couldn't remember how it began.

He'd never heard the process discussed in St. Lazarus'; he suspected it wasn't practiced, implying that no one alive was qualified to attempt one.

However, he no longer believed completely in God. Five hundred years was a long time to maintain blind faith, and the gargoyle had failed. Nothing the gargoyle had seen convinced him God existed, or that He cared, unless he counted this punishment. But what said his fate had been different than that of any other? When this stone body finally crumbled into dust, would he just move on to another body, either stone or flesh or something else entirely? Could the gargoyle even practice as a priest with these thoughts so prominent in his mind? Could he bless water or reject the angels of hell? Could he deliver a sacrament or even serve mass? He might go through the motions; but since he no longer believed, did it matter?

He'd hardly performed as a priest in life. As Inquisitor, judge and executioner, he'd spent little time serving God.

<hr />

Father O'Leary remembered the first time he'd walked into St. Lazarus'. It was huge, especially compared to the cabrini he'd served the five years before that. Even now, some ten years later, he didn't know the names of all his parishioners. He felt no guilt over this; in New York City, though more faces crowded the streets, people existed mostly in isolation. The church, or at least this particular church, was not as important a part of the community as in his hometown. New faces appeared weekly; others never returned. Here, there were too many distractions. Too many people didn't take time to stay and chat after mass. Those who did seemed mostly his parents' age, or parents of children on the path toward their First Communion.

He'd walked into St. Lazarus' expecting something large, but not so grandiose; what struck him most were the particulars of the architecture. He'd grown up in a church where the walls were thin wood, the pews tiny and humble. Here, the altar alone was the size of his childhood church. It intimidated him. The cathedral rose far higher than he'd dreamed.

The sculptures which encircled the walls—both inside and out—amazed him. Here, there were gargoyles twice the size of men, a life-sized statue of

Christ in marble, stained glass windows on either side of the church, and one huge spherical window set behind the altar depicting Christ on the Crucifix. Statues of Mary and Joseph flanked the altar, and a pipe organ reached up toward heaven. The spires towered over surrounding buildings; here, the city was old, and nothing within three or four blocks stood as high as the church. And a life-like gargoyle stood above the huge double doors which opened onto the city.

Acclimating to his new environment had been easy enough, but something about that particular statue always struck Father O'Leary as odd. It stood out, more fully rendered than the rest of the friezes; indeed, it was the only statue of a gargoyle inside. Outside, there were many statues. Inside, the other gargoyles were only mosaics and carvings.

There were times, in the midst of a sermon, when Father O'Leary thought the gargoyle actually listened. There were times, alone, when he thought the gargoyle watched him.

All this time, he'd been right.

He knelt before the altar but had no prayers to say. The gargoyle's story swirled his head, intertwining with the woman's confession of ghosts and demons. If a gargoyle lived—and, according to lore, the gargoyle existed to defend the church from demons—then the girl might truly have seen something remarkable. It disturbed Father O'Leary to think demons roamed the streets. There were too many demons already: heroin, AIDS, psychotics with automatic weapons.

There were views to the teachings of the church which some priests had taken to and others outright rejected: that the Bible was not a literal translation, but metaphoric and symbolic. The stories and parables were just that, moralistic tales. That God existed, that He lived and breathed through everyone, Father O'Leary had no doubt. Did that mean He truly destroyed Sodom? That Adam and Eve were cast from Eden because of a serpent's guile? That God created all of heaven and earth in six days, and a day of reckoning would come when Jesus and his angels returned to conquer Satan?

These were symbols. Father O'Leary didn't wait for Armageddon.

But if a demon, an actual creature from the depths of hell, walked on earth, then what he believed was wrong. If a gargoyle climbed down from walls to confess its sins, surely demons prowled the ugly streets of New York.

❦

The woman—his wife, she claimed, but Gus remembered no marriage—dragged him from the girl with the white hair. She'd been the angel in his dream, which he hadn't remembered until finding her here in the park. The image returned clearly, now that he'd seen her: white hair, blood on her hands, she stood over the fallen devil, a priest beside her and a bright light shining down upon them from heaven.

"Come on, Gus," the wife said, pulling him from his chaotic memory, "let's go home."

Home was a strange word, because it had never applied to Gus' life. In the gutter between a warehouse and a deli, a mattress served as home. They dined on whatever leftovers Angie—the other angel in his life— gave them from her deli.

"We have no home," he argued. Still, she insisted. He looked back, not hearing, but the angelic girl had gone.

"I dreamed about her," Gus said.

The wife pinched his arm. Hard. He squirmed away, cried out something halfway between a word and a yelp, and looked at her. Wife, he thought. "Penelope."

"Yes," she said. "Now come on."

"I don't want to," he said. "God is coming."

"You've said that, but would He mind terribly if you ate something first? There might be a long line to get into heaven, and I'd hate to see you starve to death."

Something about that bothered Gus; how could you starve to death if you were already dead? If you weren't dead, how could you be at the gates of heaven? "There's no line."

"There will be."

He allowed her to pull him forward—again—and off the path. They cut through the trees, on a path of their own, and reached one of the streets. Roads all looked the same. Gus couldn't read the numbers on the signs anymore, and he couldn't distinguish one building from another. He found his way, to and from, by some inner radar, a guidance system God had given him to navigate. To avoid *them*.

CHAPTER FOUR

Neve avoided returning to her apartment. In the park, in the streets of the city, the presence of people created a sense of safety. The ghost didn't show itself to others.

The sun still shone; it wasn't anywhere near late. Few streaks of white clouds broke the clear blue sky. In Central Park, the sky appeared brighter, its color deeper. Maybe this was just compared to the dark shadows of the church or the corners of Neve's mind where fear and frustration gnawed. She knew exactly how to stop the ghost. She didn't know how to do it, though, and survive.

She sat on a bench. The bum's ravings lingered in her mind, specifically his stone angels. Was it the gargoyle he'd seen, or something that existed only in his head? Neve would never have an answer.

The gargoyle believed she might be an angel; she wondered, now, if he was her angel instead? Weren't gargoyles defenders of the church? Wouldn't that cast the gargoyle in the role of savior when the demon came for her soul?

She was too tired to pursue these questions; the ghost had kept her awake all night. She wanted nothing more than to embrace the warm cloak of darkness called sleep.

She didn't mean to doze on the park bench. But with the absence of distractions, exhaustion quickly crept up on her.

In a dream, Neve stood at the edge of an alley. The demon stood above her, blood dripping from its claws. Its red eyes focused upon her, and its spread wings blocked the sun's light.

"Leave me," she said.

Its deep laughter vibrated her bones. It leaned closer, displayed sharp and jagged teeth. She didn't flinch. In her peripheral vision, she saw bodies strewn about the alley. The bum was among them; his impaled body slumped against the brick wall, held upright by a twisted street sign. All but Neve were dead.

The demon reached for her. Twice her size, with palms the size of her head, it plucked Neve by her waist and lifted her into the air.

Its hot breath singed her flesh as it examined her. The demon turned her over so that she saw the bloodied ground. Bodies filled a dumpster beneath her.

It tightened its hand, pressed the edge of claws against her skin. She trembled, but showed no other fear.

"You can't have me," she told it.

"I," it said, its voice echoing with the voices of legion, "shall have whatever pleases me."

"No!" she screamed, kicking and flailing her arms. It dropped her. She landed on her feet and began running.

The ground was slick with blood, but nothing stopped her. She ignored the rows of dead women on either side and fled down another alley.

The shadow of the demon remained above Neve as it followed. She tried to open doors on the sides of the alley, but all were locked and unyielding.

The demon snatched her from the ground. She struggled, but this time the creature held her fast. It rose into the sky, high above the tallest buildings. "I shall show you heaven," it said, "so that you may better understand hell."

She woke with a scream, alone on a bench.

She left Central Park quickly. There was no sanctuary, not even in her dreams.

She wandered without direction, disregarding the scene around her. Buildings? Trees? She didn't even know. Were there people? There was no ghost, no demon. Nothing else mattered.

Even the church, sacred and Holy, hadn't keep the ghost away. Maybe the ghost posed no threat. But its presence alone threatened her, a constant reminder of what she'd failed to do. At least the demon promised to take her away from this world, to remove her from the vicinity of the ghost. Could hell truly be worse? Would she feel as exhausted as she was now, once dead?

She wasn't resigned to death. She wouldn't surrender her soul without a fight. But she had no weapons to fight the teeth and claws of the demon. She couldn't flee from a creature who could take to the sky to chase her. She couldn't flee a creature that pursued her in her dreams.

A storefront caught her eye. The window was tiny, crammed between a fruit stand and one of those jewelry shops sporting cases of ten dollar rings in the shapes of snakes and skulls.

An angel had been etched into the window. A dozen books crowded the display, with simple titles like *Angels*, *UFOs*, and *Dreams*. There was no store name, no awning, only this small window and a door with blackened glass.

She pushed in. Cinnamon filled the air. Overlapping posters papered the walls. A dozen different wind chimes hung from the ceiling. The lights were dim, supplemented by a dozen candles on the front counter. The store was barely ten feet wide and maybe twice as deep. There were shelves of books, in no apparent order. Small wicker baskets held variously colored crystals; little white labels said Amethyst, Quartz, Citrine.

Under the glass counter, there were clear crystal balls, azure pyramids, wands with rocks on the end. There were tarot cards and pairs of silver balls in red cases. Packets of incense leaned against the old cash register.

Behind the counter, a woman with black hair wore liquid velvet. Her eyes grabbed Neve instantly: they were violet, the color of the sky at the moment after sunset. The woman smiled, a genuine beaming smile which threw Neve off guard.

Neve returned the smile and walked to the closest bookshelf. She scanned the titles, recognized none, and found nothing on gargoyles.

"May I help you?" the woman asked. Her voice was like the cinnamon in the air: sweet, slow, and thick, the perfect antithesis to the demon of her dreams.

"I don't know," she said.

"I think I can," the woman told her. "I'm Selinda Sheare."

"Neve Spirito."

"Snow spirit," Selinda said. She came out from behind the counter, picked a book off one of the other shelves, and flipped through the pages. "I can't offer much, actually. I can tell you the importance of platinum, but I haven't got much in a Christian sense. I do have Bibles, but that's not going to help you."

Neve stared at this woman. Petite, she stood maybe an inch or two over five feet, weighed possibly a hundred pounds. Hair and clothes flowed around her like a magician's cape, moving with perfect synchronicity. Something about her eyes, the color of twilight, scared and excited Neve.

"Here," Selinda said, handing the open book to Neve. In the middle of the page, a sketch showed two creatures embraced in a death lock.

Neve read the passage aloud. "The gargoyle, in service to its Christian Lord, defends the church, its home, from hell's demon. It is a battle both lose, for their immortal souls dissolve into mist. The gargoyle succeeds in his charge, destroying the demon. But the demon also succeeds, because now the church is left defenseless against the demon's son."

It made no sense that this stranger, emerging into the shadowy world in which Neve found herself, would choose the one passage which applied so well. It disturbed her, but also thrilled her. Though the creature haunting Neve had separated her from the rest of the world, it hadn't isolated her. If no one else, at least Selinda knew. Neve wasn't completely alone. She hadn't been abandoned.

"That's about it, I'm afraid," Selinda said, closing the book as she took it. "Anything else says less. But I do have something you need."

She shelved the book and disappeared into the back of the shop. Neve hadn't noticed the swatch of black velvet separating the front of the store from a second room. She followed Selinda.

Here, candles burned more brightly and there was no electric light. A candelabra sat upon the table; each of its five ornate silver arms held a white candlestick. There was less order here. A round wooden table centered the room; everything else seemed haphazardly thrown in boxes.

"Here," Selinda said, reaching into a box. "This, I think, will help you." The object, bright and long, glimmered in the dim, unsteady light. Neve leaned closer. *A cross.*

"Platinum," Selinda said.

"I can't afford that."

"Don't be so sure." Selinda held the cross before her, dangling from two fingers by its chain. Four inches wide, seven long, its end concluded with a blade, like a knife. A crown was etched into the top of the cross; the arms twisted around themselves, as though individual strands of platinum had been woven together. It might stab Neve if she wore it.

"It's ancient," Selinda told her. "I've had it back here for years, because I've never met anyone who needed it." She proffered it. "Take it."

"I can't," Neve said.

"Hold it, at least," Selinda insisted. Neve took it. The sudden weight dragged her hand down when Selinda let go. The chain, too thick to be worn as jewelry, was the same platinum as the cross. She held it closer to her eye; it caught candlelight, shimmering, and almost glowed. It felt warm in her hand, not cold as she expected.

"It was given to me in Europe," Selinda said. "Paris, I believe." She chuckled. "The man was a lunatic. At least, I thought that then. He told me about a creature which chased him, part man and part beast. He described it as a wolf with a man's eyes, a man's soul, but without a man's mind so that it couldn't reason. He told me nothing about how he came to possess this cross, except that it came from a priest whose father had used it decades before." She paused. "He never told me his name, just that the creature had finally struck his home, taking son and wife, leaving only his infant daughter. He'd hunted the creature for three years, with this and a shotgun, and finally found the man who was the creature during the middle of the day. Without the protection of the moon, the hunter thought he had the creature at his mercy, but that wasn't the case. The creature transformed before him, tore away the shotgun and the man's hand. He thrust this weapon, which you hold now in your hands, into the creature's belly, killing it, leaving him dead and in human form. The man fled through the streets. He found me, eventually, after wrapping his wounded arm in his shirt, and said, 'You need this, you'll need this next, I can see it in your eyes!' He told me the story, and I listened because I knew there was something of truth there amid his lies. I listened, also, because I knew I needed the weapon, I needed its protection, and no one else offered it to me. There was no cost to me, so there is no cost to you. Consider it a gift." She paused. "I ask only one thing."

Of course, Neve thought. Here, she'd begun thinking this woman might be sincere, that the helpfulness which exuded from her might be honest. And, of course, something lurked behind that. Neve waited for the ridiculous *one thing* which she suspected to be nothing less than her first born child.

"Wear it until you've used it."

Selinda swept past Neve, through the velvet curtain and into the main part of the store. Neve followed, carrying the cross.

"Wear it?" she asked, emerging through the curtain. There were no other customers. "Just wear it?"

"As I said, there was no cost to me." Selinda climbed behind the counter. "You need it more than I. I've used it already." She spun to face Neve again. "Yes, there is one thing more than just to wear it. When you're done, and you'll know when you're done, pass it on. You'll know who needs it when you meet them."

Neve set the cross on the glass counter between them. "I need this?"

"Absolutely."

Selinda smiled, sat back, and offered nothing more. Neve stared at her for a full minute; Selinda gazed back as if examining Neve's soul. The idea of having her secrets laid bare for Selinda struck Neve in an odd way: first, she was shy. Why should she reveal herself to a stranger? But there was also the feeling of excitement, something raw and maybe supernatural. Something of an exhibitionist grabbed Neve's mind and wanted, even needed, to be spread open for someone else to see.

Selinda leaned forward suddenly; Neve, no longer able to look in Selinda's eyes, stared at her lips instead. "If you trust no one else," Selinda said, "at least trust yourself. Look at your situation, see how you'll benefit from having a tool, a weapon, such as this. It is a weapon, remember. It kills; it has before, and it will again."

Neve sighed. She didn't want to listen, but she couldn't leave. The cross tempted her.

"If you want," Selinda said, "I can tell you something about how I used it, but I know nothing about how you will use it. Just as you don't."

Neve didn't want to trust her. "Tell me."

Selinda smiled. "I was a child, just learning my strengths and weaknesses. I have many of both, but at the time I knew little. I looked into the mind of a man who had struck me as something more than myself, more than anyone I'd ever met, on the streets of Paris. The man immediately realized that I sought something through his mind, so he sent me images. Vile, disgusting images, which I don't care to describe. Sexual and bloody, involving him and me, and at the time I didn't know if he sent these images or if I glimpsed our future. I had gypsy blood, and though I'd never seen anyone's future, not even my own, I had also never known anyone who could cast their thoughts into another's mind.

"He refused to release me. The images lingered, twirling and enveloping every thought of my own. I couldn't force him out, so I ran through the night.

"His thoughts stayed with me as I ran, though he didn't follow. He'd done as much as he wanted, as much as he needed. Yes, I had stolen a few thoughts, random things, from his mind, and only one that mattered: he was a murderer, or would be, and he was on his way to London. Somehow, I wasn't his type. I didn't sell myself. That's what he wanted, so he just left these thoughts to plague me.

"When the crazed man gave me that weapon, I thought at first it might destroy these images. I searched for days, but never found my tormentor. Indeed, I wanted to find no man ever again, because of the scenes with which he'd contaminated me. Vile, horrifying, deviant and very full of blood. After weeks of these images, during the day and within my dreams, I couldn't deal with them anymore. I pressed this cross against my chest. I doubted I had the strength to kill myself, but the shape of the cross burned itself into my chest. I felt no pain, though it looked like there should have been plenty, but the images still persisted. If anything, they strengthened. I don't know how he did it, even now, but the images gave me no peace.

"Another day, and I could deal with it no longer. I was in London, now, unable to locate the bastard, and I finally slit my own throat in an alley. As I bled, the images dissolved with the rest of the world. It wasn't quite what I expected, but it's what happened."

"You're a ghost?" Neve asked.

"No, no," Selinda said, "there are quite enough of those without me. No, I was born again a few decades later. Same body, my memories intact and only my own. I found the cross in my backyard when I was seven."

Neve closed her eyes a moment, unable to look at Selinda, not caring whether she should believe the story; the woman distracted her. Everything, now, distracted her, but Selinda was worse: beautiful, mysterious, she held the knowledge Neve wanted.

Neve felt Selinda's hand against her face, soft and warm, gently stroking her cheek as though wiping a tear. "Tell me," Neve whispered. Her voice trembled. "What's happening to me?"

Neve kept her eyes shut; Selinda's whispers sounded an inch from her ear. "I'm sorry," she said, "I don't know that." She removed her hand, and a rush of cold replaced her touch on Neve's skin. "The war between good and evil has always been fought, and never won because of exactly what the book said: good conquers evil, evil conquers good. When the battleground clears, it begins again anew."

CHAPTER FIVE

Chloe woke when the sun set. She walked to the large window of the apartment daddy's money provided and looked out onto the city. It, like she, came alive with the night.

She looked down at her fingernails, admired the bright glossy red that still didn't need to be touched up, and smiled. They might never need to be touched up, because there was no polish on her nails. Red was now her natural color.

Lipstick, though, she needed to apply; she used her reflection in the large mirror over her fireplace to do so.

Chloe walked through her rooms naked. The touch of evening on her flesh exhilarated her, and not for the first time, she wished it was acceptable to walk outside without clothes. But that would attract too much attention; as much as she enjoyed the moonlight, she couldn't have mortals too interested in her.

In the back of her mind, she knew this was a dream world. Daddy's money might disappear one day, but she wasn't worried about it; she had her own money, tucked away nicely in a big brick bank downtown. She knew the undead walked the earth, but she wasn't one of them. Yet. She hoped one of the eternal men of night would find her, take mercy on her soul, and grant her everlasting life. She yearned for the kiss of the vampire to make her one with the night. Until then, she lived as close to that ideal as possible.

She'd tried blood once; she had no taste for it. The vampire's desires and needs came with the change.

Chloe hated waiting alone, though. Rick was good to her in a lot of ways, and good for her, but lately he'd been acting strangely. He didn't phone as often. He disappeared more frequently, and for longer times. She knew there were other women—sex toys—in his life. It didn't matter, because he always came back. She had her own little toys. As a vampire, they were a prerequisite.

She examined her body in the mirror. She hadn't been out in sunlight for months, maybe over a year, so her flesh glowed blissfully pale. She stroked her arm, watching herself in the mirror as though she watched someone else; two years ago, she'd graduated high school wearing pink cardigans and fluffy whites. Now, there were no colors in her wardrobe but black and red. She had tasted irresistible darkness.

Chloe pulled on some black leather—as little as necessary—and left the apartment.

A five minute cab ride later, she rang Rick's doorbell. He buzzed her in without using the intercom.

Rick's building had her sense of style: dark, dank, tight, and crooked. She climbed creaking stairs to Rick's second floor apartment and walked in without knocking.

He sat at the kitchen table, in the dark, drinking Absolut from the bottle. "Hi," she said, using everything she could to be seductive: she lowered her voice, put on that Kathleen Turner huskiness, and glided toward him, presenting her chest and lips and hands. She wanted to go straight to bed, skip over the small talk and foreplay, skip the going out and drinking and whatever else there was. She wanted to rock his world, shake some sense into him. Make him scream, and scream beneath him. His newly developed sullen attitude frustrated her.

Rick didn't even blink. He pulled a flask from his pocket, opened it, and filled it with vodka. "Let's go." He got up and walked to the door.

"Go where?" Chloe asked. She was too startled to be offended by his rejection.

"Out," he said.

She followed Rick downstairs. He'd been moody lately, given to outbursts of shocking silence, violent at times, full of anger at others. He hadn't always been like that. Used to be, he was the smart one. He was the funny one. His wit was all but gone these past couple of weeks, ever since he'd returned from his last trip.

Was there another girl, Chloe wondered. Was there someone whose body he wanted more than hers, someone whose curves were smoother and lips fuller? What would happen if Rick left on one of his trips and never came back?

⚬━━━⚬

The gargoyle grew restless. The years that had already passed were nothing compared to the hours, the minutes, which remained before the sun set.

There were patrons in the church. One man spoke, waving his arms enthusiastically, to an amazingly patient Father O'Leary. Three elderly women gathered at the candles, praying for their departed husbands, their daughters, their sons. The gargoyle wanted to hear none of this.

His thoughts turned to the woman, her flight from the church and the ghost which pursued her. The demon she'd seen may very well be real: something in the city which preyed on the weak, stealing their souls for hell's collections. The gargoyle wanted to ensure she didn't join that army.

He knew he might be part of that army, having been denied heaven. But he didn't believe she deserved to serve eternally under Satan's fist.

She might still be an angel. He didn't know the purpose of that, but he allowed himself that hope: Magdelina, revived, returned to aid him into heaven. It was the perfect fuel for a legend, he thought, a tale to be told for generations. But he had no one to tell, and neither did she, except perhaps the other angels in heaven and God.

It was far more likely that she was his daughter. Even with five centuries between them, he could think of her in no terms other than daughter, lover, and angel.

The demon was real. Maybe the gargoyle trusted the woman's eyes because they were like Magdelina's. He would have believed anything she said. He'd follow her to the corners of the earth, to make sure the demon couldn't take her. If he couldn't stop the demon, if it did claim her soul, then the gargoyle would descend into the depths of hell and overcome Satan himself to release her.

He gave hardly a thought to his own soul; he had been reborn into this stone body, as guardian, and must do what was intended. How could he die, since he was already dead and needed no breath?

There were few reasons to remain in the church. The structure, itself, was Holy; no demon could enter, and therefore no demon could threaten the church. The battle against Satan's angels needed to be taken to the streets, where the masses who were not protected by the grace of God might find protection under the wing of a gargoyle. This could be the sin of pride; he couldn't save everyone everywhere. He had a city: this one, New York. He had a time: now. He couldn't even save every soul that walked these streets, but if he could save just one, just hers....

He hoped his daughter's soul was not beyond salvation.

He flexed his fists, tightening and loosening the stone in utter silence. The women never looked up; the man talking to Father O'Leary was too involved in himself to hear anything over his own voice.

The gargoyle wanted to spread his wings, rise to the sky again, and soar above the city. He wanted to be free of the cage which was this church. The cathedral reminded him, in too many ways, of the deep vaults in which he'd imprisoned so many heretics.

Time had taught him that heresy was a myth, that he alone carried the burden of that crime. Regardless of the accusation, the people he burned to death had committed no crimes. He, however, murdered 464 times before taking his own life—a sin in itself. Each crime worse than the last, compounded by his misguided belief that God sanctioned these actions. Would God sanction his actions today when he took to the streets in search of a demon?

Only three parishioners remained in the church; the gargoyle kept his eyes shut and knew this by the sound of their heartbeats. Their hearts' rhythms intertwined like thunder.

Father O'Leary was no longer in the church; like the gargoyle, the priest waited, probably in the rectory, for the last of the day's worshippers to leave.

A charge flowed through the air. The people couldn't smell its sharp, sweet fragrance. Father O'Leary surely did. And though the gargoyle smelled nothing, the scent came to him through his fingertips—talons— and through his wings. It was, for this church, for Father O'Leary and the gargoyle himself, a day of change.

The doors of the church flew open; the gargoyle looked down, but it was not his angel. It was a man, off the streets, whose heart beat twice as fast as any other. "God is coming!" he yelled. "He's sent his angels!"

A woman followed, tugging at his arm. "Gus, listen to me," she whispered—only Gus and the gargoyle heard; Gus shrugged her off.

"God is coming, He is here, and He offers salvation!"

Was he drunk? The three patrons were suddenly nervous, evidenced by their quickened breath and heartbeats.

The man didn't stumble as a drunkard, didn't falter as he strode confidently down the center of the aisle. "We shall be saved!" he called out, lifting his arms and voice to the vaulted ceilings.

"Gus!" the woman called. She remained beyond the threshold, outside St. Lazarus'.

Gus spun. "Be gone, woman! I've had enough of your sacrilege, your lack of faith! When God returns...." He stopped in the midst of his sentence. His eyes, having climbed to the gargoyle, widened. "His Angel is here!" he cried, pointing.

The door next to the altar opened swiftly; Father O'Leary emerged, staring quietly at the unshaven man. "Look for yourself, woman! God's stone angel makes his earthly home here!"

The other three, as anxious as they were, all looked at the gargoyle.

"It breathes," one woman whispered to another.

"God's stone angel, I pray thee," Gus cried, dropping to his knees and bowing his head, "take flight! Soar through the skies again and spread your message of Armageddon! Not everyone believes you!"

Father O'Leary moved through the church like water; he placed both hands on the man's back and whispered: "There is nothing to fear, my child."

Gus shook his head. "I know no fear in the face of God."

"It isn't moving," one of the women whispered, negating her friend. "C'mon." She urged her friends out with a gentle tug on the arm; the three women made their way, alongside the wall, to the church doors.

"He has sent his stone angels," Gus whispered, "I've seen its flight. I've seen the angel of God."

"You have seen," his companion said, bursting forward, "the bottom of too many bottles!"

Father O'Leary looked to the gargoyle. He offered the priest nothing: not a word, not a gesture. If this man had seen his flight last night, others may have witnessed it. There may be hundreds, perhaps thousands, waiting for God's reign to begin. The gargoyle wasn't willing, yet, to claim that responsibility.

"The Angel," Gus said, looking and again pointing to the gargoyle.

"Not an angel," the priest told him.

"God's stone angel."

"No," Father O'Leary said. "The gargoyle is no angel. He, as do you and I, waits for the angels to herald Christ's return. Only stone, he is not so different than our flesh and blood."

Gus looked at the priest. "I saw him fly." Tears flowed freely from his eyes.

"The gargoyle has a different purpose than you or I. He has a different mission than heaven's angels. He serves as guardian of the church. He protects those who believe." The gargoyle restrained a smile, though he felt one on the edge of his lips; the priest spoke beautifully, weaving fantasy and reality.

"He protects us from *them*," Gus said. "*They* have followed me here, I'm afraid."

"They?" Father O'Leary asked.

"There is no they," the woman said. She stood over Gus with her hands on her hips, her back to the gargoyle. "Father, forgive him. He's a drunk and a fool."

"Not a fool," Father O'Leary said, smiling at the woman, "not because he's witnessed a miracle. We all, every day, bear witness to miracles. Some are more memorable, or more obvious, than others."

She pulled Gus to his feet. "Still, a drunk."

"I've had not a drop," Gus said sharply, "not since what I've seen."

"Then perhaps the gargoyle offered this vision to you," Father O'Leary said, "to help you defeat the demon of alcohol." Again, the gargoyle liked the priest's reasoning, skewed as it might have been.

Gus looked again to the gargoyle. "Will he fly again?"

"Perhaps he will fly tonight," Father O'Leary said.

———

Gus allowed Penelope and the priest—he was a good man, after all, honest and sincere and probably right about everything—to lead him out of the church. He stole one last look at the stone angel, whose wings had spread over the New York City sky just one night before. He hoped to watch its miracle of flight once more; already, sunset approached.

The sounds of the city usually annoyed Gus: babies crying, sirens, taxi horns, and men screaming over their construction machines all day and night. But the noise couldn't penetrate his shield now; God protected him.

"Now," the wife said, "can we go and find something to eat? I am so hungry."

"Sure," Gus said. He recognized her as one of *them* now; she'd hesitated before entering the church because, though not forbidden from sacred ground, *they* found it distasteful, even painful, to walk upon. Her words were a mixture of kindness and frustration. She wanted to guide him into temptation, into the arms of Satan himself. Gus knew, now, that no traps she could lay would hold him. The stone angel, the priest's gargoyle, defended him. Drink was no demon; drink had chased demons away. But he couldn't hide behind the shield of cheap wine to survive Satan's schemes. Better to confront the devil, face to face if he must, to overcome him.

Gus followed the woman to whatever trap she led him. She'd tried to divert him since he'd awakened, clear-headed and with the vision of stone angels vivid in his memory. She sought to throw those memories away. She tried to chase away his dreams, of the woman with the white hair, of the angels, of the coming of Christ. She failed. Consistently, she failed. He had the might of God, the might of Jesus Christ, on his side. "Lead me not into temptation," he whispered, "and deliver me from evil."

Peace was an outdated term. Chaos and anarchy loomed on the horizon. The second coming of Christ brought Armageddon. Satan would walk the earth, to be finally defeated. And all of *them*, who followed Satan and held him close to their hearts, would fall with their evil lord. The wife, too, would fall; Gus, and the few who knew Christ as their true savior, who had heard the call of angels—stone or flesh or clouds—would ascend into the kingdom of heaven.

They crossed another street. Here, there were others like him, dressed in rags, dirty, and beaten. Life had been harsh, and heaven's angels soon came to redeem them.

There was food here; this was the place the wife had tried to lead him all day. No trap pounced. Maybe while the sun shined in the sky, the minions of evil couldn't freely walk about the earth. If she was one of them, though, this couldn't be true; maybe, under the light of day, they had no strength, and so only a few ventured into the sunlight.

They had to send someone to lead him to the slaughter. Unfortunately, *they* didn't understand that, with God's imminent return, it was *they* who would be slaughtered. Slaughtered, and banished to hell.

Early evening light filtered through stained glass. Gus, raving by any onlooker's description, had gone, and with him the remaining visitors. The priest stood at the open door, looking at the city streets. The gargoyle bent to watch, gladdened by the long shadows which stretched off the church to a good height on the building it faced; the day neared an end.

Anxiety gripped the gargoyle. He had no heart, yet sensed—rather than felt—its racing beat as night approached.

Finally, Father O'Leary shut the door and turned his attention to the gargoyle. "He saw you?"

"He may have."

Father O'Leary walked slowly down the aisle; he cast his gaze upon the other statues and engravings. The Virgin Mother didn't move to console him. Christ didn't climb down from his cross.

The gargoyle was too high for the priest to see clearly in the light of candles. Regardless, Father O'Leary turned and examined at him.

An eternity passed. The gargoyle noted the slight tremble in the priest's hands and his shallow breaths. Finally, Father O'Leary asked, "Do you wish to be seen?"

"It was not my intention," the gargoyle told him.

"What, then, was your intention?"

The gargoyle removed himself from the wall. This prison tired him. He desperately wanted to flee into the night. He longed to taste the freedom of flight.

"My intention," the gargoyle told the priest, settling directly before him, "was to ascend to heaven. To join the Father, Son, and Holy Spirit and walk through the Garden of Eden. To speak with angels." He crouched, so that his head was level with the priest. "My intention was to leave this mortal earth, this stone body, and join my beloved Magdelina on the other side of heaven's gates.

"I never left these walls before," the gargoyle continued. "I never knew I could. Until the white-haired angel came, I had neither strength nor will move. My first night in the world, last evening, I rose through the sky and tried to meet God. This city dwindled to a dot on the planet, and then less, as I rose higher and higher toward heaven." Already Father O'Leary had diverted his accusatory gaze, but the gargoyle was not done.

"I never saw the gates of heaven. I can't ascend into heaven in this body, not until I fulfill whatever role I'm here to serve." He paused, where as a man he might have taken a breath. "I must serve my angel."

"And how do you intend to do that?" Father O'Leary asked. "There may be no demon haunting her."

"I *have* seen her ghost."

"And the demon she believes watches her." The priest inhaled deeply. "Your soul, your mind, was condemned to the body of a gargoyle. Does that imply there are demons? When I spoke with her, when I listened to her confession, I was sure the demon and ghost were creations of her imagination, her own mind haunting her. I told her as much."

"I heard every word," the gargoyle said. "I don't know if there are demons. I have never seen one. But I do know everything else she claims to have seen exists. I have seen the ghost. I, myself, am the gargoyle. Did you believe she'd actually seen me move?"

The priest smiled. "Of course. *I* have seen you move."

The gargoyle stammered. "What?"

"Sometimes, I thought I imagined it. Late at night, alone with only the light of candles, I thought it was a trick of the light. When she said she saw you move, I had no doubt. It confirmed my own beliefs. But the other things; these, I thought, were created by an imagination inspired by you. The ghost, you say, is not her imagination, and so I trust it is not. But nothing substantiates a demon."

"Just," the gargoyle said, "as nothing substantiates a God."

The priest's smile grew and he shook his head. "Life substantiates God. I need only open my eyes to see miracles all around me. Open those doors, take a good look at the world. Look at the mothers who give birth to our next generations. Look at the trees, the clouds. Breathe the air, so you can see and feel and taste and smell miracles everywhere."

The gargoyle laughed. "I can't breathe the air," he said. "Still, you put your faith in an idea you have not personally seen. Neither you nor I have seen God's hand come down and create; we have seen only the creations, and attribute these to a God our grandparents learned of from their grandparents. Father, you place your faith in something invisible, something supernatural, and yet you cannot accept someone else's faith when she claims to have seen, with her own eyes, a glimpse of another world?" He leaned closer to the priest. "I'm not suggesting you are wrong with your faith, merely that you are wrong to deny the faith of another. And if a demon walks on the earth, and I walk upon the earth as well, does it not imply that I am here to aid her against this thing?"

After a while, the priest sighed, "Perhaps."

"You may be right," the gargoyle added. "The demon may exist only in her head. But even there, it's something I may be able to vanquish. She is the blood of my blood, like an angel delivered to redeem my soul. Even if she's not my Magdelina."

"You may expect too much from her."

"I expect nothing," the gargoyle said, "but a chance to redeem myself. If not in God's eyes, or even Magdelina's, then at least in my own."

The gargoyle looked up at the stained glass. Little light broke through the dark hues of the window even at midday; but now, as evening settled upon the world, only the dim candles provided any illumination.

"She'll return," Father O'Leary said.

The gargoyle turned and extended his wings fully; they stretched six feet in either direction. On the floor, they almost brushed the tops of the pews. "I can't wait for her," he said. "I must go to her."

"And what if you don't find her?" the priest called out. The gargoyle, at the front doors of the church, ignored the question. "What if more people see you?" Father O'Leary asked.

St. Lazarus' doors opened onto New York. The last light of day dimly tinted the busy street. Automobiles and people were everywhere. For a moment, the gargoyle considered Father O'Leary's last statement; here, three or four dozen faces were but a twist of the neck away from watching him emerge from the cathedral.

The gargoyle moved too swiftly for anyone, in the dying light of day, to clearly see.

The doors swung shut behind him; the gargoyle perched at the highest spire of St. Lazarus', among the outdoor gargoyles.

The one nearest him was as fully sculpted as he, complete with the distorted face of a lion and the hands of a man. No wings. It gave no indication of awareness.

Here, the gargoyle appeared to be just another part of the architecture. He scanned the immediate area, unable to find his white-haired angel. Unlike Father O'Leary, he didn't expect her to come to the church. She had seen enough. She was not an angel, by strict definition; God hadn't send her upon a mission of mercy. She was no reincarnation of his lost Magdelina.

Yet, the gargoyle had no doubt that she was an angel, his angel. She was his blood. She was his flesh, and Magdelina's, reborn. He wanted nothing more than to speak with her, comfort her, show her how harmless the ghost which haunted her was. Defending her from whatever demon she might have seen could begin to make up, in his own mind at least, for the wrongs he had done.

The gargoyle soared into the air. Though he felt nothing, he heard the wind rush past and imagined what it might feel like going through his hair or over his skin. Once, he'd been human. He curled his talons into fists, so tightly that he heard stone grind, as his wish for blood and flesh strengthened.

The city was huge, and the world beyond it was much larger than the world in which he'd lived. Christopher Columbus had opened up the new world in 1492; the gargoyle knew nothing about this until four hundred years later, when he heard the whispers of churchgoers in this "new world." He had explored a hundred square miles during his dream flights.

But awake, in the flesh—or stone—the world loomed larger. More people crowded this one city than had existed in his entire world. Too many faces resembled each other. One of these endless faces was his angel, child of his children. Through her, he hoped to make peace with Magdelina. With himself. Failing that, he hoped to at least bring peace to his angel.

Father O'Leary sat in the front pew. At forty-nine, he was too old to have his faith shaken like this. Demons? Gargoyles? Ghosts? In the world in which he'd grown up, these things existed only in fairy tales and campfire stories.

Could this gargoyle redeem himself? Father O'Leary could never commit the gargoyle's sins. The world was different then, so he couldn't imagine how he might have acted in the same situation. He knew only what he needed to know about The Inquisition: people died. Was it important that his church had sanctioned these murders?

The gargoyle intended to help his angel, regardless of the consequences to her. Father O'Leary believed she'd return when she was ready. Instead, the gargoyle had gone to search for her. If he found her, the gargoyle would only frighten her more. Never in his life had Father O'Leary seen anyone with so many reasons to be frightened. If a ghost haunted him, and demons stalked him at night, he didn't think he'd be as strong as she was.

He stood, crossed himself, and left the church to eat dinner.

<hr />

Rick tapped his fingers on the steering wheel. Next to him, Chloe quietly examined her long, red nails. They were the same bright, vibrant color of her lipstick; she had no other colors except in her eyes: hair was black, clothes were black. But her eyes were an awesome green, a richer shade than money. Her face was pale; he didn't think she'd seen the sun in months, maybe years.

Chloe fancied herself a vampire. She believed the black leather contrasting with her pale skin made her exotic. And maybe it did, a little. Rick couldn't remember—or didn't want to—if she had ever been beautiful. Now, she looked like little more than an overused cartoon, a cheap Elvira with smaller breasts.

Rick glanced at her. She looked at him and smiled nervously. "What?"

Rick coughed a monosyllabic laugh and returned his gaze to the speedometer. It sat at zero.

"You've been all weird, past couple of weeks," she said. "What's up with you? Where's your head?"

Rick laughed again. "The clouds, Chloe. The clouds."

She leaned closer. There was a time, not so long ago, when her touch excited him. Now, she was only good to empty himself into. He used to care about her. He used to worry. But he couldn't concentrate on her anymore, could hardly look at her. He didn't understand the change. Yes, there was a time when he'd thought she was the most beautiful creature to roam the night. She was his Angel from hell, his vampire lover, until his white-haired angel of mercy had failed him.

"Let's go, then," she whispered, using that deep, sultry voice that, once upon a time, had turned Rick on. "Let's visit the clouds."

"I have another idea." Rick started the car and

pulled into traffic. Peripherally, he noticed a taxi miss him by sheer luck.

"Where we goin'?" Chloe asked.

"Church."

Chloe laughed, maybe because she didn't think he was serious. He offered no explanation. When they finally reached the church and climbed out of the car, she hesitated as he bounded up the stairs.

He almost hated her, but knew that wasn't true. It couldn't be. "What?" he asked.

"I don't think I can go in there."

"You're crazy." He pulled both doors open.

The church was quiet, empty. There was no priest. That's not what he needed. He pulled an empty flask from his jacket. He'd already emptied it in his throat. Opening it, he dunked it into the dish of holy water.

Chloe came closer. "What are you doing?" she asked.

He splashed some at her. "Preparing," he said. She cringed from the water, slapped at her arm as if it burned, but of course it didn't.

"You're not gonna try and kill me, are you?" she asked. That deep voice again. He wished she'd shut up and leave him, let him do what had to be done. It was almost time. The change was almost over.

"Maybe later," he said. He stepped deeper into the dark church. No candles burned. There was only the streetlight from the door Chloe held open.

"I'm not going in there," she said.

"Don't," he told her. "Hold the door." He walked to

the altar. Years must have passed since the last time he'd walked into St. Lazarus', but it still held vivid memories for him. His father would point at the priest and say, "He'll be gone before you're old enough."

The church doors shut as he reached the altar. Finally. His elation was short lived, though, because when the echoes of the door's closing fade, footsteps followed.

"Thought you couldn't come in," he said.

"I can," she said, "I just don't like it. Gives me the creeps. Catholic school, remember?"

He found the chalice filled with communion wafers. Hoping they'd already been blessed, he popped three or four into his mouth and shoved more into his pocket. He knew they wouldn't stop anything. Just as his avenging angel had failed to stop him. This, he knew, had been his last attempt to avert his destiny. If angels and holy communion wafers failed to strike him down, his role on earth must really be important.

"Ever know something?" he asked, leaving the altar.

"What do you mean?"

"I didn't think so." Rick threw the church doors open and jumped down the steps.

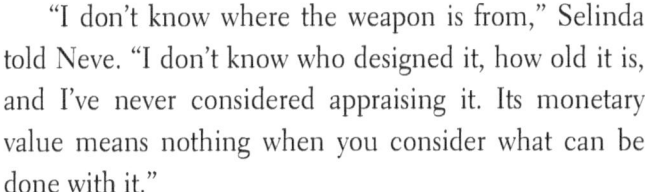

"I don't know where the weapon is from," Selinda told Neve. "I don't know who designed it, how old it is, and I've never considered appraising it. Its monetary value means nothing when you consider what can be done with it."

The glass counter separated Neve Spirito and the shopkeeper. Black velvet protected the windows, guarding the inside and outside from each other. No one walked through the door, and no city sounds penetrated what appeared to be thin walls and flimsy windows.

The platinum cross and its chain lay on the counter, catching the dancing candlelight.

Neve saw a comparison between this shop and the church; both relied on the light of candles and the faith of believers. There was no church if not for the strength of the parishioners' collected belief. There was no store if not for the money of its believers. The Bible was similar to any book on these shelves, relating stories which supported its specific point of view. In the case of the Bible, it professed God and Jesus; here, the books might have concerned government conspiracies, the secrets to exploring dreams, or the hidden powers of the mind. The stories were not very different.

Many of the relics within these walls were religious in nature; the platinum cross was only one example. Numerous books on Catholicism and other religions lined the shelves. Here, as in the church, there were Bibles. And, as the priest preached in his church, Selinda preached in her shop.

The only difference in Neve's eyes was that most priests believed what they preached; people in Selinda's position believed more in the power of the dollar.

"Nice shop," Neve said, turning her back to the woman and eyeing the wind chimes, crystals, and candles. "Not too busy, though, are you?"

"Business," Selinda said, "is not what keeps me in business. Sometimes, but only sometimes, there is someone who truly can benefit from what I have to tell them, what I can show them. You, I believe, are one of these people. You may not believe me now, but when you look back, you'll realize what I'm saying is true. The cross is yours. It's a weapon, a key, and a symbol. Go, use it, give me nothing but your promises in return. I acquired it at no cost, and pass it on to you."

Neve turned around; the space between them seemed to have decreased. "Why should I trust you?"

"Do I ask you to sacrifice anything?" Selinda asked, placing the cross in Neve's hand. "Do I request compensation? I don't even ask you to believe anything you don't already believe in: God, your soul, the power of Good over Evil. What is there not to trust?" She didn't release Neve's wrist. Her touch was warm.

Neve didn't try to pull away. "I'm nervous."

"Of course."

"You make me nervous," Neve said. "I don't know why. I have enough to worry about." She closed her eyes. "Do you have any idea of what I've seen?"

Neve sensed Selinda's lips as she talked; they were soft, pliant, an inch from her own. "I know," Selinda said. "You know what you must do."

"I suppose I do," Neve whispered. She felt her breath strike Selinda's flesh; they were almost close enough to be one person, united in spirit and body. Neve's pulse raced, and she tightened her fist around the cross. "Thank you."

Rick got out of his car. No lights brightened his apartment. The window was open, but the blinds were down so all he saw were white stripes on black.

Chloe slammed the car door. "Rick!" she said.

He turned around. "What?" He wanted to love her still. He wanted to hold her, draw pleasure from her touch. He wanted to kiss her. His mind was a jumble, and it no longer mattered whose body he touched, whose touch he felt. He continually flexed his fingers, tightening and loosening both fists. "What?"

"What's going on with you?"

He turned back to his apartment. "Nothing."

She ran to him, swung her arm hard at his shoulder. "Don't lie to me!" She pounded his chest two, three, four times with both arms. Rick ignored her. He wondered if anyone, or anything, could hurt him at this point.

"Upstairs," he said, shrugging off Chloe's attack and climbing the stoop. Chloe stared at him from behind.

"Something's wrong with you," she said. "You're not you."

He opened the glass apartment door, kept his back to her. "No one is."

She didn't follow him inside, and he was relieved. He keyed into his dingy apartment building, climbed the dark, narrow staircase, and didn't look back. It was better if Chloe left. He had thought he loved her, but now knew he wasn't capable of love. His legacy denied its existence. There was lust, there was hatred, there was anger. He hoped something in the church might have helped him, but maybe only a priest could have helped. Or maybe the priest would have only further driven his bloodlust.

When Rick was a child, his father brought him to church every week, sometimes twice. Dad pointed certain things out, things which went mostly unnoticed by the congregation. "That statue," he said once, "is alive. He doesn't know it himself, but it's his job, his mission, to protect the church from demons."

Rick looked down at his hand as he opened the apartment door. His father was gone, flying across the world or something. Or maybe he was right here in New York, doing his job and doing it well. Rick never had a mother; at least, not one he remembered. Always, it was the two of them. There were women in Dad's life, coming and leaving in incredible numbers: three, four a week, sometimes two in a night. Some simultaneously. Dad always allowed Rick to watch.

One of Rick's earliest memories was of some blonde handcuffed to the thick wooden bedposts. She screamed at Dad, begged him to hurt her. She writhed in pain and pleasure with every strike of the whip. Blood seeped from her chest in rigid, straight lines. More wounds bled on her back and ass, and she'd loved it.

That was the thing, Dad always told him: "Get the ones who want it. They deserve it most."

In a way, maybe that's what had attracted Rick to Chloe. She lived for death, sought it in her recklessness. She longed for and feared it, so she worshipped it. She made herself to be a vampire and played the part well. But there were worse things in the world than vampires.

Rick went to the front window of his apartment and looked out between the plastic slats. Chloe sat on the hood of the car, examining her nails in that annoying way she had about her. "Leave, already," he whispered.

He could have told her everything. She'd believe. She might not have approved of what he thought the Body of Christ might do to him, but that wasn't her concern. He reached into his pocket, pulled out the last of the wafers; he'd eaten two dozen already, without effect. But Rick never gave up easily. He swallowed the last of them and looked down at Chloe again.

She was beautiful, regardless of what he thought sometimes. She was smarter than she let on, afraid intelligence might be a sign of weakness on these streets. She was wrong, but she wasn't smart enough to know it. An intimate knowledge of death gave her a stronger appreciation of life. She clung to death to celebrate life. The conclusion startled Rick.

He did have a mother once. She died in childbirth. Dad told him everything: how much blood there was, how his mother screamed and cried. She had feared the baby, because she knew it would kill her. She knew, before he was born. It saddened Rick, to think his mother sacrificed her life to give him his; she'd made her sacrifice in error.

Chloe might be a mother one day. Dad knew this, and for that reason he never said anything about her. He frequently reminded Rick there were other women, even if only for a night or two. Rick needed no encouragement. Last week, he'd finally shown Dad his trophy room.

Rick had set up a huge warehouse out in Brooklyn, almost completely empty except for a single desk. The building dwarfed the massive ten foot desk. Mahogany. Dad always said it was better to do with than without. Rick converted the office into a workroom. Here, he'd set up mirrors on two walls and the ceiling. Gymnastic rings hung from the ceiling. A four poster bed, with handcuffs attached, was propped against the mirrored corner. A wood and glass shelf system displayed a variety of rings: gold, silver, diamond. Friendship rings, school rings, wedding bands and engagement rings. Gems of all types were set into these forty-three rings. These rings had been the lives he'd taken. In a way, these had been their essence.

Each symbolized something different, something essential, which had belonged to the woman whose finger they'd hugged. No beginning. No end. Sometimes a stone or an engraving served as a focal point. They were important. The rings embodied his victims and maintained their presence in his life. He loved every one, and hated them, as much as he loved and hated Chloe.

His father had given Rick the first ring: slim gold, plain, unremarkable, it had been his mother's wedding ring, the only thing she left Rick or his father. The centerpiece of the display.

His first kill. Other than Rick, she'd left nothing else to the world.

It was like a brother.

He chose his victims as Dad had always suggested, taking the women who wanted it most. They courted death without caution, and he'd answered their call.

"Impressive," Dad said, but nothing more.

A computer sat on the desk; Dad's handwritten filing system was archaic and monstrous. Rick kept details Dad could never keep, like scanned photographs and identification. A second phone line connected him to the Internet. He spent hours there, days at a time, and always Chloe waited for him without questions.

She hadn't seen the trophy room yet.

She still sat out there, waiting. But now, she had started to ask questions. Rick understood. He claimed to have loved her, convincing even himself. But if he loved her, what was the point of the trophy room?

Chloe was a good girl. Confused, perhaps. Scared. But basically good, and that frustrated Rick. Her act was just that, an act; she didn't have the heart to be a vampire. Still, she embraced that lifestyle and all that came with it—including Rick's frequent trips.

But there came a time in every man's life when everything changed. Puberty, some might say, but Rick passed that a decade or more ago. This was a different change, something more complete and unique. He couldn't have Chloe near him while the change happened. Even if it took a year or more.

Dad's change had taken only a month. It had been about that long for Rick now, why wasn't it over yet? His stomach churned, and a dull pain ran up and down his spine. The sunset invigorated him. He hadn't slept in twenty-seven days. He hadn't eaten in twenty-three, until tonight's communion wafers.

The effects of the holy communion disappointed him. He wanted dramatic change. He wished he could be with Chloe forever, to love and marry her. He had the ring. He wanted to tear down the trophy room and drive a stake through his father's heart—this, he knew, was Chloe's influence.

None of that would happen, because nothing could change what he was. In time, he would accept it. When the change was over.

SINS OF BLOOD AND STONE

CHAPTER SIX

Gus stood at the corner. He didn't notice much of what was around him. There were signs, people, taxis, and buses, but the sounds didn't register. The wife was gone; when she'd fallen asleep, he'd slipped away from her and her trap. No longer would he be led around by some woman—or any of *them*—to some undesirable fate they'd arranged. Instead, Gus wandered the nighttime world. He looked often to the sky in search of the stone angel.

The priest had told him the angel would fly tonight. Priests couldn't lie. It was against some doctrine or something. Gus wanted to go back to the church, but he wasn't sure how to get there. He tried, three times, to ask for directions, but *they* ignored him. At least *they* didn't stop him. Without the wife burdening him with half-truths and outright lies, he was free to wander until he found the angel. Or until the angel found him.

"Hey," a voice called to him. He turned toward a child, wrapped in a leather jacket and topped with short, spiked hair. A cigarette hung from the kid's lips, and he leaned against a blue mailbox. "You," he said, nodding his head toward Gus.

"Me?" Gus asked. "I ain't got anything." There was no nervousness. He didn't know what the kid wanted. He might have come to deliver a message to Gus, perhaps a message from God Himself.

The kid pulled a deep drag off the cigarette and said

through a cloud of exhaled smoke, "Don't matter none."

Gus stepped closer. "God sent his angels."

"Yeah, yeah," the kid said, walking into an alley.

Darkness swallowed the kid. He didn't ask for anything, didn't threaten Gus, didn't even contradict him. Okay, his words were thick with sarcasm, but Gus was intrigued. He followed the kid.

Next to a dumpster, the kid dropped his cigarette and crushed it under the heel of his boot. The white tee shirt underneath the jacket almost glowed.

"What?" Gus asked.

"Did I say follow me?" the kid asked.

"No."

"Then tell me, old man," the kid said, "why'd you follow me?" The kid circled Gus, looked up and down the length of his body as one might examine a newly bought car in need of work.

Gus remembered driving a car once, a green rusting Ford station wagon that had lived a lot longer than it should have. He didn't remember what happened to it. Did it finally cough its last? Did its engine cease, or did Gus sell it before it was too late? He had no money to show for it. Maybe someone had stolen it, the car or the money.

The kid was suddenly an inch from his face, screaming. "I asked you a fuckin' question, old man!"

"I don't remember," Gus told him. "It used to run, but maybe I sold it. I don't know."

The kid hit him, hard, in the jaw. The shock of pain brought Gus back, completely, into the present. He tasted blood on his lip, but somehow remained standing.

The kid hit him again, in the stomach. Gus folded over with an odd, guttural sound.

"I don't like you," the kid said. He hit Gus again, a knee in the jaw. Something in Gus' face cracked. The force threw him on his back.

"Stop," he pleaded. He couldn't see the kid. The whole alley blurred. Blackness crept in on the sides of his vision. He tried to stand. The kid was there again, virtually invisible in the haze of Gus' vision, hitting him in the face. Hard. Very hard. Something in the kid's hands now. Not just a fist. Something solid. Cold. Heavy. Gus swallowed a tooth as he dropped back to the ground.

His ears rang. He couldn't understand the kid's shout. He closed his eyes, because the trembling cement wanted to make him sick. "Stop," he tried to say again. The word didn't quite escape his mouth.

The kid grabbed Gus by his clothes and yanked him to his feet. Gus struggled to stand on his own. The kid spat words into his face: wet, sharp, cold. Their actual meaning, even their sounds, eluded Gus.

One eye saw only a blanket of red. Something was wrong with it, something bad. He felt nothing there: no pain, no heat or cold, no blood or sweat. His other eye saw the kid's outline. Details were too difficult to make out, blurred and distorted. Something stood behind the kid. Probably another kid. Probably a dozen others.

They had pushed him in this direction, led him to

this alley so *they* could beat him until he died.

When he died, at least, Gus would finally witness God's glory. He'd die with a clean conscience. He didn't fear death, just as he didn't welcome it. He thought he had more to do, that he might witness Christ's arrival from heaven. Instead, he would see Christ's departure.

The kids—surely a dozen, an unnecessary amount for an old bum such as Gus—moved closer. The one who held him turned and screamed.

Gus blinked. Blood showered him. The kid's blood. The thing behind the kid was something else. It was no angel. Gus tried to back away and stumbled. The kid's head fell to the ground, and then the body. The creature stared directly at Gus.

The creature moved closer to him. Swiftly. Frighteningly. Too fast for Gus to focus. His eye wasn't focusing anyhow. An eternity passed between the creature's first movement and its lifting Gus by the shirt.

The creature licked blood from Gus' face. Not all of it, just one stroke with the tongue. It burned Gus' skin. "Jesus is coming," Gus tried to say. The words were jumbled in his mouth, but the creature understood.

"There is no Jesus," it whispered in a hauntingly deep, throaty voice. "There is no God."

Gus smiled. The creature released him, and Gus fell to the ground. He didn't know, as the world grew dark around him, if he'd wake up in the alley or in heaven.

Midnight approached; Chloe still sat on the hood of Rick's car. She didn't understand what was wrong with him. He wouldn't talk to her anymore, wouldn't submit to her advances. Wouldn't even kiss her. It was either another girl — but Rick was the type to have three or four at a time, so why would that stop him from kissing her? — or something worse.

What was worse? Drugs, maybe. Some drugs were bad. She avoided those whenever she could, though certainly she was no stranger to them. She knew which ones were safe and which weren't. Maybe Rick had gotten into something really bad, something unfamiliar to her. Maybe he was sick and needed a doctor. But doctors didn't visit places like this, wouldn't see people like them, so she desperately hoped it wasn't a doctor he needed.

Did that mean she hoped it was another girl? By process of elimination, maybe. Chloe stopped looking at her nails and turned her attention to Rick's dark window. Was that movement? Did he stand there, watching her? Did he back away when she turned toward him?

She jumped off the hood and climbed the stoop. She stroked the concrete railings with her fingers as she walked. Only three feet high, they didn't provide much protection against falling to the basement level below. She liked the feel of concrete. It held and embraced the cold, just as it captured heat. It existed with the world around it, changing with its environment. It held ice during the winter, burned your hands in the midst of summer. When the sun fell, it cooled under the light of the moon. It reminded Chloe of herself.

She rang Rick's apartment. He buzzed her in. No questions, no comments, as though she had just arrived. Drugs, she decided. What else would make him forgetful like that? Something good, she was sure, maybe something expensive so he didn't want to share it. Didn't he know she could afford the best money could buy, and bought them all whenever desire struck?

She reached his apartment and pushed the door open. She walked in slowly; there were no lights, and she didn't see Rick in the kitchen. She locked the door behind her and crept through the tenement. "Rick?" she whispered. She'd never realized how loudly she walked. When the blood of vampires coursed through her veins, there would be no sound with her footsteps unless she required it.

"Rick?" she said again. She walked toward the front of the tenement, through two rooms before reaching the bedroom. Two windows looked out on the street. Rick stood, with his back to Chloe, at one of those windows.

"The night is beautiful," he said.

"Of course it is. It always is, to me." She stepped closer. Rick put out his hand, as if to say stop.

"There's something you need to know," Rick said.

"Another girl?" Chloe asked. "Some chick you met on your last trip?"

Rick laughed. "No girl could take me away from you," he said. *That* was the old Rick talking.

"Then what?" Chloe asked. She was five feet from

Rick, but his hand was still up and something about it prevented her from moving closer. There was something strange about it, something different; was his hand bigger than she remembered, or was it a trick of the light?

He turned his face toward her, to show Chloe the luminous red eyes which had replaced his own.

Chloe stared at those glowing red eyes for a long time before saying anything. "Cool."

"No," Rick said. As he moved closer, his eyes returned to normal. Hair rose on the back of Chloe's neck, as though she should be frightened. This was Rick, though, and there was nothing to fear from him.

"I want it," she said.

"There's no such thing as vampires," Rick told her, touching her arms. "It's not something I can give. Not to you."

"Not to me?" Chloe asked, shaking his hands off and stepping away. "Not to me!? You can give it to that other chick you go off and fuck all the time, is that it?"

Rick shook his head, and turned away. "I can only give it to my children."

Chloe stared at his back. His shirt had been ripped by the muscles which bulged, clearly visible, underneath. He always had a body, but the sharpness, the definition of his back muscles—even without light—had become unreal. She moved closer, put a hand through the tattered shirt to touch his flesh. It was hard beneath her fingers, tight and warm. The muscles rippled as he breathed and talked.

"I've given this a lot of thought," he said. "I want you to be the mother of my child."

"Excuse me?"

He turned, slowly so her fingers never left his body. "I need an heir, and he needs a mother." She stared open-mouthed at him. Nothing indicated that he might be kidding. "I want you to be that mother, Chloe. I love you."

She closed her mouth, swallowed. She tried to say something, but only stammered "I" a couple of times.

"Tonight," he said. "We can do it tonight."

She grinned. Even if he wanted it just to have a baby, at least he finally showed some interest in sex again. But what if she did get pregnant? Daddy's money would disappear then, that was for sure. Rick couldn't support her, not without stealing. Eventually, her own money would run out, and she wasn't exactly the working type.

"Tonight," he said again. He stroked her cheek, softly, tenderly, as if he really loved her. She wondered at that, but didn't resist when he moved his hands down to her jacket and then her shirt. With a slow fingernail, he tore them open.

"Yes," Chloe said, shaking off the ripped jacket and shirt. She wore no bra because she wanted nothing of restrictions. The air chilled her breasts.

She wanted him, needed him. She couldn't wait. She threw herself forward, into his embrace, and found his mouth with hers. She surrendered completely. Dark pleasure flooded her when he ripped what remained of her clothes. She pressed into him, pulling at his clothes. He was larger, now: his arms were bulkier, his chest was wider, his mouth opened more, and his tongue felt longer as it entered her kiss. She felt him, pressed hard against her, from the middle of her thigh to her belly button. Something about him had changed, and she didn't care what had caused it. She thrived on this.

Their sex was raw, painful at times. He was too big to be inside her, and yet he pushed completely in. He touched her everywhere, as though he had more than just two hands. Of course, he only had two hands, but they were larger, their fingers longer, their grip firmer, and their flesh rougher. His mouth never stopped, hungrily kissing her everywhere. He threw her against the wall, pushed himself up and into her further, and she couldn't help but scream with the pleasure. His body was like warm, flexible marble. Hours, days, years later, he spilled into her. Waves of orgasm rippled through her. Very hot, his seed boiled inside her.

Exhausted, she collapsed against the wall.

Rick carried her to the bedroom. Gently, he laid her on the bed and drew a blanket over her. Even the touch of the silk blanket created shivers of pleasure. He'd unlocked her senses, so that even the smell of the night thrust her into ecstasy.

In a way, she finally knew what it felt like to be a vampire, to be truly alive. Sleep quickly claimed her in Rick's bed, where she dreamed of the things they'd done, the things they could do next time. It had been unlike any other time, with Rick or anyone else, and all the terms—sex, making love, fucking—failed to describe what Rick had done to her. It was a little of all of that, and a lot of something else, something unearthly, that drained her energy, even in her dreams, but Chloe had an endless supply of energy, and so the dreams continued, each image more powerful than the last.

CHAPTER SEVEN

When Chloe woke, she was alone. She sat up, savoring the aches in her thighs, arms, and back. Her torn clothes remained where they'd fallen; Rick had left his jacket on the bed for her.

She ignored it and walked to the window. She felt more alive, closer to the vampire, than ever before. She leaned toward the window, hung from the top pane. This displayed her breasts, intentionally, for whatever eyes might glance in her direction. Eyes should never be disappointed.

Cars lined the side of the road, and a few moved through the night. Half a dozen people walked out there, wandering one direction or another.

No, there was no other. Everyone traveled in the same direction. The cars, too, moved in that direction, or was it some odd coincidence? Rick's car was gone.

She left the window. She felt no desire for blood; milk satiated her thirst. Half a carton slid swiftly down her throat, cool and energizing.

She looked around the apartment and squinted. Did she see better in the dark tonight? She felt stronger, of that she was certain. Despite aching muscles—or perhaps because of them—she felt better than she'd ever felt before.

She didn't know what Rick had become; he said vampires didn't exist, and he couldn't gift her with whatever he was. He could give it to his child, and he sounded almost desperate to have one.

Chloe chuckled. She wanted no children. She wanted to be, eternally, a daughter of the night. She couldn't be bothered with maternity, with an infant to raise. She touched her stomach, and stroked the softly rippled texture of her abdomen. There was no room within her womb for a child.

She returned to the window and pulled it open. Less than a dozen people walked in one direction. She shoved half her body out the window and called to the nearest couple. The man was scrawny, too tall, and the girl only a little less than Barbie doll perfect. "Where you going?"

The man looked up at her, surely seeing erect nipples on the ends of her fist-sized breasts. The girl looked, too, with something of contempt but nothing of envy, and immediately Chloe hated her.

"Party!" the man yelled back.

Couldn't be a party without one of the undead, Chloe told herself. She climbed back into the apartment and looked at Rick's jacket on the bed. She felt completely invulnerable, but knew enough to wear something. She put the jacket on, leaving it unzipped so it covered her breasts but would easily reveal them with the proper twist. She wanted—needed—to be noticed. She searched Rick's closet and found a pair of jeans. Not her color, but in the dark everything was black. She looked at her fingernails, again amazed that they were so perfectly colored, and stopped in the bathroom to check herself out.

A comb through her hair, water on her face, and Chloe was ready to party.

She took the stairs three at a time, pushed the apartment door open, and entered the most highly charged, energetic of nights. Electricity crackled in the air, waiting for the proper outlet. "Yes," she breathed, jumping down the stoop.

The air cooled her skin, but she knew several ways to warm it. She saw only three or four people on the street now, no moving cars. She followed the crowd. Soon, she heard the music. It carried on the air like a surfer on the ocean. The odor of beer and cigarettes and other smoke welcomed her.

An entire apartment building housed the party. There were no tenants, no furniture, no lights but the candles people had brought. There were drugs aplenty, everything possible. A few deep kisses, in special places, got her two of her favorite little pills. What would sex with Rick have been like on these? It was impossible to guess; the pills never had affected her as strongly as Rick tonight. She couldn't get his body out of her mind. Always, Rick had been strong and muscular, but tonight he had switched his body for that of a weight lifter, and yet it remained his in every way. He had tripled the size of his penis and doubled the length of his tongue. How much of that was Chloe's imagination, delusions brought on by her desires?

She danced on the stairs, throwing her eyes across every man and woman not hidden by shadow. She doubted she'd recognize the vampire if one had come, but she did know she'd find someone with whom to have her own private party. Man, woman: it didn't matter. All were delectable to a vampire's palette.

She didn't know where the music came from; it was nothing but a heavy beat, all instruments and voice lost somewhere within the walls. The building swayed with the party. Chloe felt danger in the air, anticipation which she hoped would lead to one thing.

The party helped Chloe forget Rick. She couldn't forget his size, ferocity, or passion, but she lost the callousness, coldness, and uninterested look which recently plagued his eyes. Uninterested, not just in her, but in everything.

She forgot all that, allowed the music to move through her, and soon even forgot there were other people here. She had taken one of the pills and felt strong enough to tear this building apart brick by brick. It flowed through her veins, pushed her feet to dance as though there was no exertion. Sweat poured down her body, gleaming in the light of candles. It caught the cold air, accentuated it, but she felt none of that.

Chloe danced from one floor to another. Up the stairs, she kissed any man and woman along the way. Not everyone, just any pair of lips close enough to hers, any mouths between where she had been and where she was going. There was no destination, just climbing.

Higher, the music became more complete. Shrill highs and screeching vocals joined the thunderous bass in a cacophony of noise. It breathed through her. She never felt so close to the darkness, so at home in it as now. A combination of the setting, candles, music, and drugs. More, it was the residuals of Rick's sex which drove her.

After three flights, Chloe ran out of stairs at the roof. There were people here. The music came from somewhere downstairs now. There were no candles, only the dim moonlight. She looked up into the sky, at the stars and sliver of moon, and wondered if she could fly. She had always wanted to. With a vampire's blood in her veins she would fly, but Rick was no vampire. He was something worse. She didn't know exactly what that was, or how anything compared to a vampire as "worse." No, mortality was worse; anything more was simply divine.

An awkward boy stood near her, some blond staring at her and not dancing. This jacket beautifully displayed her breasts; his eyes riveted there until he realized he'd been seen. He turned away, embarrassed, and tried to disappear in the crowd. But Chloe's senses were at their peak. She followed him, dancing rather than walking, and put a hand on his shoulder. He turned, pushing up his glasses nervously.

He didn't fit in this crowd. He wore one of those plain white business shirts, long sleeved, buttoned up to the neck. She wanted to feel his throat and taste it.

What was someone like him doing here? She didn't think to wonder too much. His moist lips trembled slightly. Every muscle was tense; he had been caught as he stared, and now feared his fantasy's response.

Chloe said nothing. She twisted his shirt collar in

her hand, applying only the tiniest amount of pressure to his throat. The top button flew off, bounced off her jacket. She pulled his face close to hers and kissed him.

He was so nervous, so unsure of himself, it excited her. Her tongue forced his lips apart. He could hardly kiss her back under the force of her mouth. She wrapped her tongue around his, could almost envelop it like a vampire. She tugged at his shirt, popping more buttons. He neither resisted nor helped. She twisted her body so one breast was completely exposed, and pressed it against his cold, hairless chest. Hard. Letting go of his shirt, she slowly pulled her body away. Her hands slid down his chest, across his belly, not releasing the kiss. She reached into his pants—not jeans, but actual pants—and beneath cotton briefs.

She removed her lips. She pulled her breast away from the boy and drew back her hands. Leaning close to his ear, she whispered, "I want to suck you." His blood, but she was completely aware of what he imagined. She brushed his ear with her tongue and turned away. The music's rhythm guided her toward the stairs. The boy followed.

Chloe took the boy to Rick's apartment.

The apartment was dark, and the boy's nervousness was visible. So was his excitement and curiosity. Chloe thought she'd be his first. It thrilled her to think hers might be the first female flesh next to his since his mother fed him at her breast. She shed her borrowed jeans as soon as they got into the apartment; clothes, again, just got in her way.

He stood at the door, afraid to enter.

Chloe no longer heard music, but still felt its rhythm in her muscles and bones. She danced without the sound, writhing her way out of the kitchen.

Behind her, she heard the door close. She didn't look back. She was willing to bet her soul that the boy was inside, right behind her. She nearly heard his heart beat, and felt tension exude from his flesh. She wanted him to hurt from wanting her so badly. Dancing deeper into the apartment, she dropped Rick's jacket.

She didn't expect the boy to be like Rick. She expected to enjoy nothing more than the boy's enjoyment, excitement, and pleasure. That, and that alone, could be enough for her. No man, no mortal man, could repeat what Rick had given her earlier.

She reached the boundary of the bedroom. Here, Rick had given her an ocean of orgasms, an inhuman level of pleasure, a few short hours ago. He'd given her something no mere man could give.

She turned. Something inside her said to leave the bedroom alone, leave it as a sanctum for Rick and herself and no one else. The boy stood at the threshold between the next room. Facing him, there was nothing of her not exposed to the boy now: her tight, pale breasts, sharp nipples, the blonde hair between her legs. Some of her body hid in shadow; there were no lights, and she intended to leave them off. She licked her lips, part in anticipation and part because she knew how he'd react.

The boy shook; tremble no longer adequately described it. He pushed his glasses up his nose; they slid back down. His sweat reeked of nervous excitement. She slid closer. The rhythms within her head moved her legs and body to a tune no one else heard. She touched his cheek with her finger, walked around him. From behind, she gently took the glasses off his head.

He almost resisted. His shoulders tensed, as though he might stop her, and then slackened again. She dropped the glasses softly on the couch and pressed her body against his back. She crossed her hands over his chest and pushed beneath the tattered shirt. It tore as she pulled it out of his pants. Not a single hair grew on his chest, not even the beginnings of one. She had never felt a body so smooth.

Senseless sounds escaped his mouth. She put a finger on his lips and shook her head. She guided his hand to her thighs. She moved his hand to rub herself, first on her flesh and then inside it.

She stroked herself with his hand and wrapped her other hand around his neck. Another kiss. It paled next to the immortal touch of a vampire or the inhuman mouth of Rick. But it was better, too, in that it was new, fresh, fumbling. He knew little about what they were doing. He was about to learn.

That, more than anything, excited Chloe.

His fingers were timid and shy. They didn't need the rest of his inexperience to be afraid of what they did. She taught them quickly how to touch her, where to stroke, how much pressure to apply. His confidence grew as she moaned and shuddered. Maybe he believed he was a natural lover. Maybe, after shedding his excess anxieties, he was.

Chloe removed his hand; again, he almost resisted, not wanting to stop touching her. Kneeling, she slid his pants to his ankles. He gasped as he was revealed. She almost laughed—not because of what was revealed of him, but because of his reaction—but managed to hold it back. It would be a quick end to her pleasure, and she enjoyed this boy far too greatly to give him up because of something stupid like a laugh.

Rick's apartment was cold; he always kept it that way, winter or summer. It was almost as cold as the air outside, just enough to make nipples erect and form goose bumps on arms. The boy had both.

Once he got over his initial fears, he proved to be a good lover. He was only a boy, perhaps half a dozen years younger than Chloe, but she didn't care. She didn't know his name. Didn't want to know. His method was rough and clumsy—against the wall like they were didn't help him any. He thrust when he shouldn't have, and focused far too much attention on one part of his body. A true lover would know there was more than just a cock to be shoved inside a woman. There were hands, fingers, mouths. There were places to touch, and ways to caress, which could do far more than any thrust. Still, she orgasmed beneath the pleasure of being his first. He spasmed, embarrassed at how quickly he'd lost control, but she didn't care. It was another part of him, and of his lack of experience, which had turned her on.

Done, Chloe realized Rick could return home at any time. It was one thing to have sex toys on the side; it was another to play with them in his apartment.

Quickly, she pulled Rick's jeans on and snatched the jacket from the floor. The boy leaned against the wall, exhausted. His legs quivered, ready to fail. She leaned close, kissed him roughly on the mouth, and then slapped him. "Get dressed."

The slap shocked the boy. He stared at her, bewildered, but he didn't question her. He gathered his clothes methodically. Glasses went on first, perhaps because he thought she wouldn't slap him again. Chloe watched from the corner of the room, smiling but anxious. She didn't know if she wanted Rick to come home or not. She wasn't sure how he'd react. Part of her feared for herself; what if he saw this as a personal attack on him, a dishonor which he might punish severely? She didn't know what kind of punishment a Rick with twice the muscle might deliver.

Or he might be satisfied taking his anger out on the boy. But he was only a boy. Even a vampire recognized innocence.

Waiting, Chloe reached into the jeans pocket and swallowed the second ecstasy pill.

The boy was attempting to button his shirt. Most of the buttons were gone, and the sleeves and left side were ripped. He looked at her, confused. Chloe shrugged. He didn't have to follow her here. A shirt was a small price to pay for a taste of her body, the flesh of the vampire mistress. What price might another person at the party pay? She chuckled at the thought.

"What?" he asked.

"Get out."

"But..." Whatever else he might have said, he left unspoken. He turned and left.

Chloe went to the front window to watch the boy emerge from the apartment. Her smile expanded. He'd never have another quite like her. Maybe she'd come back for him some day, after he learned something.

But, for tonight, there was plenty of time, and the party still seemed to be attracting people. She left Rick's apartment and headed back.

The cold woke Penelope in the middle of the night. She gathered her blanket more tightly around her. The cold penetrated because of the holes in the blanket, but she was used to it.

She turned slightly, to see Gus' unused blanket.

It was a tiny home: behind a dumpster off a numbered street on the West Side, the flimsy mattress served as bedroom, living room, and dining room. Three dumpsters in this alley provided a kitchen when Angie at the deli didn't, and a barrel stuffed with old newspapers sometimes gave Penelope fire to warm herself or her food.

Most nights, Gus wandered off. Always lost in his own little world, lately his world had become stranger. He talked about stone angels flying through the streets, here to cast *them* aside. He didn't know who *they* were, but *they* had always been a part of his little world. He was paranoid, and she'd lived with his paranoia all her life.

Maybe not all her life, but she didn't remember a time before Gus. Even those lost years, when she was a child—and surely, at one time, despite her inability to remember, she had been a child—seemed sprinkled with Gus when her memory cleared.

But clear memory was a luxury neither she nor Gus possessed. The mattress, two relatively warm blankets: those were their luxuries.

She rubbed her eyes and rolled off the mattress. She saw no sign of Gus. At least, she knew where he might go: that church, with that stone angel he had raved about. And what, she wondered, might he rant about tomorrow?

Chloe hadn't really looked at the party the first time, so she couldn't tell if it had changed. There seemed to be more people, or maybe she hadn't noticed before. She remembered no one but the boy—who, rather than return to the party, had probably gone home to cry because he'd never duplicate the experience.

There weren't as many candles as she'd thought; there was a lantern, oddly out of place, on the ground floor. The doors dividing the two apartments from the hallway were missing. Chloe danced through one of those doorways.

The music's beat pulsed in her throat. All around, there were people on top of people, some literally. Two men engaged in a deep, hungry kiss in one shadowy corner. Nearby, a long, thin glass pipe was passed between a circle of people. The current smoker used her lighter, and it cast almost as much light in the room as the three candles on the only piece of furniture: an old, rotten table propped against the radiator. There was no heat.

A man stood in the space once occupied by a freezer. He looked at her with fierce, dark eyes and smiled. He wore only leather, tight as skin, and smoked a Clove cigarette. He inhaled deeply, letting the smoke flow slowly from his mouth, and never took his eyes off Chloe.

Shivers dotted her spine. He had the perfect look: a body chiseled from stone, hypnotic eyes, a sinister smile. He was the antithesis of the boy. He appeared exactly as she would have her vampire lover: tall, lean and muscular, pale and handsome. He took the cigarette from his mouth, looked for a moment at its ember tip, and looked again at Chloe.

"Yes," she whispered, in response to his unspoken request. She didn't lose the rhythm. It may have been her dance, and not just the open jacket, which had attracted his attention. She refused to release—or seek release from—his eyes. She glided to him, almost a vampire herself now, and moved directly into his embrace. Confidently, boldly even, he covered her lips with his mouth.

His kiss to her was like her kiss to the boy; she felt inadequate, innocent. She tried to return the passion, tried to offer what he wanted to take, and felt that she failed miserably.

When their lips parted, she tilted her head to expose her neck. She wanted his kiss, needed his teeth to break her skin and suck the blood from her veins. Without his gift, she'd have no reason to live. No reason but Rick, but that thought was distant, all but lost in the triumph of this moment. She felt his lips on her throat, soft and wet. "Please," she whispered.

Somewhere, someone screamed. Part of this moment, Chloe thought. Someone saw the vampire's teeth as they were about to sink into her flesh. But even the vampire looked up, toward the door. The strength flooded out of his embrace, and his lips fell away from her neck.

Chloe turned, slowly, to see what he looked at. The doorway. "Rick!"

But Rick was no longer the man she'd known. He had grown even more muscular. His shoulders were twice the width she remembered. He stood outside the doorway, because it was too small to let him pass. His skin had changed from pinkish flesh to a pallid green. It was as if Rick's face found a new home on a discolored version of The Incredible Hulk. Even his eyes were different: something between crimson and gold.

He wore no clothes. Chloe wanted to shed hers, as well, and join him.

Rick walked through the door. He didn't try to squeeze his body through the opening; instead, he shattered the empty frame and sheet rock. It didn't slow him.

Chloe looked at the vampire. His mouth hung open. The forgotten brown cigarette fell to the floor. She stepped out of his embrace as though his arms weren't there. With the awed look of a deer caught in headlights, he stared as Rick's monstrous body came closer.

Everyone else existed only peripherally. People screamed, but Chloe didn't know who or exactly why. Blood dripped from the claws which had replaced Rick's fingers; had he torn through mortal flesh to reach her? She surged forward. Rick caught her and held her to his side as he advanced on the vampire.

He carried Chloe so that she could see the frightened expression on the false vampire's face. "You *are* a vampire," she whispered to Rick.

"Not quite," Rick said. The false vampire alone was frozen in his place; everyone else ran over each other trying to get away. No other caught Rick's attention.

Rick lifted the pretender with one hand. Chloe watched Rick's muscles contract and expand. She admired the beauty of it; there was something completely awesome in Rick's transformation. She wanted to be a part of that, wanted to share whatever he had. She wanted to become what Rick was.

Rick tightened his fist over the pretender's neck, crushing it. Eyes bulged, and the false vampire spat blood. The snap of his neck overwhelmed all other sounds.

Rick dropped the limp body, and turned to look at Chloe. He drew his lips back, displaying inch long fangs.

"Take me," Chloe said, closing her eyes and offering her neck. "Make me like you."

He dropped her. When she opened her eyes, Rick was at the window. Sirens approached. He looked back. "Go," he commanded. The window and its frame shattered as he left.

Chloe ran to the hole. People, still screaming, ran in all directions outside. Blood streaked the street and the stoop. At least three people bled from massive wounds on their chests and faces. Someone had lost an arm; it lay in the gutter.

Chloe ran to the hallway. The sirens were closer, and she wanted to be far from here when the police arrived.

A dozen bodies were crushed against the bottom of the stairway. She ignored them. She ignored the fallen screamers, leapt over them without a thought. She pushed her way through the crowd; still, there were a dozen or two people inside the apartment building. Upstairs, the music still played; Chloe pictured people dancing on the roof, unable to hear the screams or sirens over themselves.

On the street, Chloe ran. Rick's apartment was little more than a block away. A cop car passed her, its lights flashing and sirens screeching. Another followed closely. Neither noticed Chloe on the side of the road.

She hopped up the stoop, pushed her way quickly through the vestibule, and took the stairs two at a time. She threw Rick's door open and stopped. She panted, out of breath, and stared at Rick—the old Rick, without the excess muscle or color or even the red eyes—sitting at the kitchen table.

SINS OF BLOOD AND STONE

CHAPTER EIGHT

The streets were a jungle to Neve, a maze with no beginning and no end. She had no direction, no destination. She feared the solitude of her apartment, so even with night settling upon the city, she roamed its streets. She stayed near people.

Twice, she considered returning to Selinda's shop. More often, she thought about the church. She touched the platinum cross under her shirt, but it gave her images of the gargoyle rather than Selinda. It was cold against her chest. She needed its comfort, its protection. It was not a ward against evil, but a weapon. When the time came, she intended to use it.

Hours had passed without an appearance by the ghost. Neve wanted to give her the justice she sought, but it was beyond her power. Neve could call the police, tell them everything she knew, and even lead them straight to the warehouse, but it would do her more harm than good. There was nothing there for the police to find; when he learned she'd revealed him, Rick would kill her.

The scene wanted to replay itself in Neve's mind — the gun and the demand, the rings — but she refused it.

Night spread itself prettily among the clouds and skyscrapers. She didn't notice specific buildings; exactly where she found herself didn't matter, as long as people surrounded her. As the streets thinned, anxiety drew its icy fingers across Neve's lower back.

Wandering annoyed her. Exhaustion gnawed at her. At least when she passed out, the ghost wouldn't be able to wake her. She wanted just a few hours of uninterrupted sleep, without the demon.

She touched the cross again. It wouldn't affect the ghost.

She realized, with a start, that night was upon her. Darkness cloaked the streets. The ghost might not bother her, but the demon's face flashed through her mind. It had watched her from an alley, and it watched her now. She looked quickly in every direction, searching for its glowing red eyes. No crowd was large enough to prevent the demon from taking what it wanted. If it desired Neve, she expected no safety in numbers, no sanctuary in the open air. Perhaps only the church offered that.

She no longer had anything to think about. The church, and only St. Lazarus', could assist her. Even Selinda's knife was in the shape of a cross; surely, that was a sign. The book from which she'd read, about the gargoyle and the demon, mentioned a church.

She forced the gargoyle's words from her mind, refused to ponder their meaning. She was no angel. A demon stalked her. It, not the gargoyle, had said her name.

Neve checked over her shoulder. Nothing. She walked swiftly now. An end was all she wanted, not understanding. She wanted statues to remain solid stone and for demons to retreat to the pages of Bibles. She wanted ghosts to fade into projected movie images, harmless and unreal. She needed sleep.

The pews of the church might not be comfortable, but she knew no other place to go. Sleep might elude her, regardless of where she made a bed.

She hailed a taxi. During the ride, she counted the minutes. She lost track after five.

So many times in the past weeks, she had climbed those steps and walked through those doors. After stepping out of the taxi, Neve stopped to look at the outside of the church. Here, the carved gargoyles were more realistic, more finely sculpted. There were a half dozen: two over the doors, one in every corner, and hundreds of smaller ones scattered throughout the walls of the church. Spires brought the building closer to heaven. No windows faced this street.

The violet sky was a velvet blanket; few clouds scarred its perfect color. A whole universe existed up there, and heaven as well, yet the demon had chosen her, Neve Spirito, to stalk.

Perhaps Rick had conjured the demon to watch her, to make sure she kept quiet. She easily pictured him lighting candles and reading Latin from dusty scrolls. She even saw snakes twisting in a circle drawn with human blood on the floor. The demon rose from the ground, emerging between the lines of a glowing pentagram. "Watch her," Rick commanded, and the demon obeyed.

Neve closed her eyes and forced the images out of her head. She wanted nothing less than to relive that night.

The images flowed.

Handcuffs, blood on the girl's wrists: they swirled through Neve's head, intermingling with the imaginary ceremony. The girl might have been there for days, weeks even, chained to that bed. As if still there, Neve saw the desk, the computer, the shadows. She saw the man himself, smiling and laughing, leading Neve into the converted office which held the girl.

Neve, shutting off the memories before they replayed themselves completely, climbed the steps of St. Lazarus'. The doors stood open. She walked into darkness.

The priest knelt before the altar; he, and no one else, occupied the church. Neve had expected to be completely alone. She hesitated.

"Please," the priest said, turning slowly, "come in."

◦———◦

"I'm Father O'Leary," he told the woman. She was the gargoyle's angel, identical to a woman five centuries dead. Reincarnation was not an idea Father O'Leary believed in. When Magdelina died, she faced her final judgment, and resided now in either heaven or hell. She had not returned in the body of this woman, whom the gargoyle found so alluring.

He understood the gargoyle's feelings toward her. She was exceptionally beautiful, and probably more striking when she wasn't so badly in need of sleep. Dark circles underlined her bloodshot eyes.

"Neve Spirito," she whispered. She looked up, to the gargoyle's position on the wall.

Father O'Leary had avoided making any phone calls. He should have reported the gargoyle to a number of places, the cardinal first among them. Something had stopped him, some belief that God directed the statue and the ghost. This girl, Neve Spirito, came here because he, Father O'Leary, could teach her something. And he might learn from her. Together, they could exorcise the demons which haunted her head.

He firmly believed the demons haunted only her head. Perhaps the ghost was an angel.

Again, Father O'Leary saw the holes in the gargoyle's story. Conveniently, the gargoyle had no memory of four hundred years of punishment. He wouldn't confide his name. Anyone reading about the Inquisition could have told the gargoyle's story. He trusted only himself and his observations, and only maybe did he trust God anymore.

Father O'Leary couldn't discern the gargoyle's motivation. Seeing none, he had no choice but to take the gargoyle's words as fact, momentarily, but the concept of demons chasing women through the alleys of New York City didn't sit well with him.

"He's out," Neve whispered, turning to him. "You know?"

Father O'Leary nodded.

The gargoyle settled on top of a bridge. Far below, trucks and cars rushed by. Darkness hid him from their eyes. Far beneath them, black water reflected the night.

Dawn approached, and he'd failed to find his angel. Had she already served her purpose? There were millions of people in the city; if he ventured too close to any, someone with more influence than a drunkard might expose him. Invisibility was essential to avoid persecution. The gargoyle knew the fervor which could be inspired in man; one man had passed it to him once, and he'd spread it like a plague over the entire countryside. More people lived in the world today, and hysteria's strength lay in numbers. Revealed, the gargoyle would be hunted and destroyed; no place in the world would provide sanctuary.

He imagined the destruction which would follow his discovery. The people, as a mass, had no conscience, reason, or intelligence. They acted on whim and on the will of others. In their hunt for the living, breathing—not breathing, actually, but no one would care—gargoyle, no church would be safe. Cathedrals across the world would topple, to prove this statue or that statue didn't hide the deformed soul of a sinner. It was hubris to assume no other gargoyles existed, so discovery would sacrifice not only his own soul, but the souls of every other statue which housed former men. Houses of worship would crumble, brought down by hand and machine, fire and misconception. The Pope himself might condone the action, as he had once condoned The Inquisition.

To cause that destruction, to risk the lives of others who remained silent and motionless, was too much for the gargoyle. Rather than continue his failed search, he left the top of the bridge and flew back toward St. Lazarus'.

The air was still, broken only by his flight. He flew as low as he dared, searching faces for the countenance of his angel, her flowing white hair and beautiful blue eyes.

He couldn't imagine what thoughts she must have. She'd heard part of his confession, but how much? Had fear of the gargoyle driven her from the church this morning, or a fear similar to that which prevented the gargoyle from revealing himself to the world?

It would take no effort for the gargoyle to fly into the television studios and have his image beamed into the boxes of every citizen of the country. He could bring his search to the public, plea for his angel to return. Television was one of those things he never could have imagined five hundred years ago; he understood, now, why he'd had the ability to travel in his sleep: to wake to today's world after having lived in such a morbid time as his own, the gargoyle would have crumbled under the weight of alienness. Everything was so different, how could he have had time to think about his angel when confronted with buses, trains, and buildings which scraped the sky?

He reached St. Lazarus' before the sun rose. Father O'Leary woke, startled, against the altar. "Finally," he said, stretching.

The gargoyle glided, just above the floor of the church, to the altar. Under the steady beat of two hearts, the gargoyle heard the doors swing shut behind him. He listened carefully, to be sure he was right. Yes, he heard the calm rhythm of two people's breaths.

Father O'Leary stood as quickly as he could, smoothing his robes. "She came shortly after you left."

The white-haired angel slept on the floor of the altar, curled in a ball and wrapped in a blanket so that only her white hair and three slender fingers were visible. He wanted to move closer, but suddenly the priest stood between them. He spoke in a whisper. "She needs sleep," he said. "She'll stay when she awakens."

The gargoyle stared at the perfect shape under the soft, wool blanket. "She is Magdelina reborn."

"That, I don't think," Father O'Leary said. "Her name is Neve Spirito. She asked me to stay so her ghost wouldn't wake her. She needs sleep."

"I don't remember anyone sleeping on St. Lazarus' floor," the gargoyle said.

"Unique circumstances require unique solutions. She wouldn't have slept if I hadn't promised to remain. I couldn't let you come back without knowing she came looking for you."

The gargoyle smiled; he didn't know how it looked to the priest, who saw his grotesque features stretch into something which was supposed to be pleasant. The gargoyle had seen his face in the mirrored windows of plenty of buildings across the city, and easily saw how it may have frightened his angel — Neve Spirito. He would have been frightened, had the face belonged to another.

Without taking his eyes from Neve, the gargoyle asked, "Why did she come back?"

"I think," Father O'Leary said, "she expects you to defend her from her demon."

⚬────⚬

Another day, the gargoyle agreed, was not too long to wait. Against five hundred years, a single day more meant nothing.

Father O'Leary shook Neve Spirito awake as the sun peaked over the horizon. He ushered her across the altar to the anteroom. "You can see me, I can see you," he said, "so the ghost won't come. But I have to give mass, and you can't be sleeping on the altar."

Silently, she agreed and fell quickly back to sleep on the couch. The priest left the door half open and returned to the church. Morning mass was a couple of hours away, but some worshippers arrived far earlier than that.

The gargoyle settled in his position standing guard once again over the church. He hoped it would be his last day of service. His angel slept now, but when she woke, what miracles might she reveal?

"She's sleeping again," Father O'Leary said.

The priest was an unusual ally; since the gargoyle's disservice to the church—following the commands of the Pope, though he might have been—he expected neither assistance nor understanding from anyone. And yet, this priest whom he had watched for ten years, who had watched him for as long, offered solace and even forgiveness.

They'd never completed his penance, the gargoyle realized.

The church door opened. An elderly woman ambled painfully to the altar. She walked slowly, though she had no apparent inability. Her hair was white, unlike Neve's in every other way.

The woman was Mary, as in the Virgin Mother. She came to St. Lazarus' every morning, staying through mass and sometimes longer. She crossed herself before entering the church, and again before taking her usual seat: the aisle, third pew from the front on the left side. Sometimes, she left a quarter, lit a candle, and said a silent prayer for people who lived only in her memories. The gargoyle knew much, through observation, about most of the regulars.

Morning dragged. The sermon seemed short, almost hurried. No one noticed but the gargoyle. He kept perfectly still, watching worshippers wander in and out.

He listened, throughout, to Neve's breaths. They were short, steady, and comforting. Twice, her heart rate increased and she breathed more heavily. Dreams — nightmares—disturbed her sleep, but failed to rouse her.

Remaining motionless frustrated the gargoyle, though it had never bothered him before. He wondered if Neve Spirito had granted him the freedom to move.

She may have given him that power, but more likely she had only given him the desire.

The urge to move, to go to her, plagued the gargoyle throughout the day. Hours stretched, filled with far too many minutes. He learned to hate time as the day lingered. He learned to fear waiting. If a fire started, if a war broke out and took this church before the gargoyle could speak with her—this type of nonsense contaminated his thoughts, for none of these would happen. Even God couldn't be so cruel as to tease, and Satan had no place within the church.

Laying on a soft couch, Neve Spirito opened her eyes. Dim light came from the partly open door, which led to the altar. She sat up, touched the cross under her shirt, and looked around the sparse antechamber.

The shade was drawn, allowing very little light through the window. She saw no clock, and didn't even know what day it was.

She remembered sleeping on a park bench. Had she slept there an hour or a day? She felt so much more relaxed now, as though someone had lifted the weight of the world from her shoulders. She remembered dreams, images from them at least, but they weren't as bad as the dream of the demon. Neve remembered Selinda, and how distrustful she had been. Why? If she'd had a reason, Neve no longer remembered it.

There were two doors in the room. One led to the altar, and through it she saw the priest speaking with two elderly ladies and a small boy. The other, closed, probably led to the rectory.

Neve rose, slowly, and folded the blanket. She hardly remembered walking into the church. The priest had been waiting, and offered the blanket almost immediately. The gargoyle was gone; she didn't know if she should worry about or be comforted by the priest's words: "He's gone looking for you."

"Gargoyles fight demons," she'd said. Was it a question or a statement? She hadn't had the strength to make it either.

She walked to the door, careful not to make any noise. If one of the ladies looked over and saw her, there might be a scandal: "As the good Father gave us mass," the women might whisper, "he kept a floozy in the back room."

She moved close enough to the door to see the back of the church. There, over the double doors that led to New York City, the gargoyle rested. He looked directly at her, but made no movement. His arms were extended to the sides, as though he prepared to crucify himself.

Once before, she'd seen him move. She'd seen him absent from the wall. He lived.

She stepped back, sat again on the couch. Thirst and hunger struck together; how long had it been since she'd satisfied either need?

There was a small refrigerator; she poured a glass of water and ate two slices of cheese. It wasn't much, but it chased away her hunger. Or curiosity quenched it. She hadn't spoken with the gargoyle yet. She still might have been imagining all this; she might wake at home, in bed, and find no gargoyle, priest, demon, or ghost. There might never have been a dead girl or her killer. Twenty minutes of deep sleep, a dream unlike any other, and she might wake sweating but fine. Did this inspire images for her art? Perhaps, but she was too frightened to consider that; definitely, her art would change. As dreamlike as the world seemed to her recently, it more closely resembled a nightmare; she'd only ever painted the good dreams before.

Neve listened to the muffed voices of the priest and his visitors. One of the ladies seemed vehement about something. Bingo? Neve almost laughed; did that woman say something about bingo? And here, Neve thought she had problems.

When the last of the people left the church and Father O'Leary stood alone before the altar, Neve Spirito watched calmly from the door as the gargoyle lifted himself from his perch and flew to the priest. He landed soundlessly.

"How long did you watch me?" She stepped onto the altar, within ten feet of the gargoyle.

"I think," Father O'Leary said, "I'm not needed here." He turned to Neve. "I'll prepare some dinner. When it's ready, you're welcome to join me."

He left. Neve repeated her question. "How long were you watching me?"

"From the moment you first stepped into St. Lazarus'," the gargoyle said. He drew his wings in and sat back to make himself as unimposing as possible. "It was early evening. The sun's light no longer penetrated the stained glass, and you came quietly and quickly into the church. Your heart raced. I watched you pray, as I have watched a thousand people pray over the past century. But you were different."

"I'm your daughter," she said, remembering his confession. "Your daughter's daughter, if we go back far enough."

"Only five hundred years," the gargoyle told her. "Time stretches much further than that."

She smiled, sitting on the pew, and said, "Have you seen the demon?"

The gargoyle shook his head. "I have seen your ghost. I was a ghost once; for four hundred years, I returned to the same grave, and could only tell her I loved her."

"Magdelina's grave," Neve said. "I heard that much."

"The point of which," the gargoyle told her, "was that I could only speak. I returned to that spot at intervals, but had no control. I have no memory of where I was when not at Magdelina's grave. Never once did I see people. Not once did someone see me."

"It's different for me," she said. "She returns to me, not to my grave." She paused. "That doesn't mean I'm about to die, does it? Is she waiting?"

The gargoyle shook his head again. "I don't know all the answers. I would think, though, you were present at her death, and so she returns to you rather than a place. Wherever you are, so long as there are no others. I saw the ghost because she didn't know I was sentient." He looked from one side of the church to the other. "She doesn't return now because it's obvious that I am aware."

"She comes, but not because I was there when she died. I wasn't." Sighing, Neve stood and walked to the rack of candles. "But I did nothing to stop it, and I could have." A dozen of the candles were lit. She wondered if telling the gargoyle how the ghost died would help. It couldn't hurt, except to bring back the unwanted memories. But they returned on their own; she still saw those handcuffs, silver stained with blood. And she still saw the girl's reflection in the mirrored walls. There had been nothing else to see, except the shelves — and that, certainly, wasn't pleasant to look at.

"I didn't kill her," Neve said.

"You don't have to tell me. But you can."

"Were you a man?" Neve asked. "Or were you once a man? What should I call you?"

"My name no longer matters," he said. "Just call me gargoyle. For more than a century now, I've been nothing else, and I have no intention of being someone else again. He, the person I once was, died five hundred years ago. I'm all that's left. No body of my own, no life, just awareness."

"Gargoyle, then." A frown crept into her face. "Listen, it wasn't pleasant, the whole situation. Maybe I shouldn't tell you, but I need to. I want to get it out of my system. Maybe she'll stop coming."

Without pause, she started her story. "He approached me at an art show. I had two of my paintings there. He told me his name was Rick, but I knew it wasn't. Still, he intrigued me. He was good to look at, articulate, and had that rough-guy look. He said he knew by my hands that I had painted 'Angel.' That was a piece I'd done in white, silver, gray, and gold: a winged woman stepping out of a cloud. He said it reminded him of a piece he'd done, a drawing, a long time ago, and asked if I wanted to see it sometime. I went with him that night.

"Maybe I shouldn't have. Maybe I should have thought a little more about rushing off with some man I didn't know. I could easily have gone home and watched TV.

"In the car, on the way to his place, he told me he knew everything about me. He knew my name, where I worked, he even knew the color underwear I wore. I didn't ask how he knew all this." She paused again. "I don't know why he didn't worry me." As she spoke, though she'd revealed nothing yet, it felt right. The story needed to be told, and Neve was suddenly relieved she had the gargoyle to tell.

What about this statue made him so trustworthy? He spoke softly, though the sound of gravel came through his words. So did a touch of Spain, but it seemed almost washed out, as though five hundred years without speaking the language destroyed most of his accent. In a way, his story was similar to hers; whereas she only witnessed the horror of her lifetime, he was a tool of it, manipulated by someone else. Only the gargoyle's words confirmed this, but she believed him. Something about his story, and the fact that he didn't try to shed his guilt, suggested that higher powers led him. Someone had given him free reign to kill, but never told him how to reign over it.

She, on the other hand, had failed to kill.

The gargoyle loved her. He tried to hide his grotesque face in the shadow. He leaned back, to be less imposing and threatening. He'd searched the city through the night for her. If not her, he loved the memory of Magdelina. While Neve was not Magdelina reborn, she might be the physical manifestation of his former lover. She was the reason he'd given up his post above the door. She couldn't help but trust him.

"We didn't travel far. I thought he would take me to his apartment, but instead we went to a warehouse. I should have known something was wrong. He said he owned it, which didn't impress me because money means nothing to me. I'd just begun my vacation. I decided to stay here, in the city, and spend the days, not just the nights, doing my stuff, visiting museums and watching art films and going to this show where Rick was.

"By remote control, he opened a garage door and we drove into the warehouse. It was empty. Completely empty." Neve paused. "No, there was a desk, but that was all, and an office. The office door was closed, though, and I wish I had never seen what was inside.

"'I collect things,' he told me. 'I want to show you my collection.' He led me to that office. 'You're my angel, my avenging angel,' he said, more than once that night. The first time, with a little wine in me and the glow of all the other artists at the show, I thought he was talking about my painting."

Neve hated the memories. They came without effort and spilled from her in quick, tiny spurts. She couldn't convert everything into words. But as the tale flowed from her mouth, the memories drained. By releasing them, she purged herself. She had to tell the gargoyle everything; then, she'd be able to sleep again — as long as the ghost never returned.

Unless the demon was something more than a figment of her imagination. She wasn't ready to surrender to that yet. She'd only seen it once, in the shadows. Maybe, hopefully, it was nothing more than a trick of the light playing on her imagination after having seen the gargoyle's first shadowy movement.

"He collected rings," Neve continued, "but he told me I wouldn't be joining his collection. 'You're my angel, remember,' he said, 'so it's up to you to save me.'

"The office was actually a bedroom. A girl laid there, on a big and pretty four poster bed. She was handcuffed to the corners of the bed. She was naked, sweaty, and shaking. She wore an engagement ring on her left hand.

"'I'll add her to my collection,' Rick told me.

"I expected to die, at that point. Seeing that girl there, crying and trembling, voice hoarse from God knows how many days of screaming, scared the hell out of me. I had no doubt that I was there to replace her.

"I was wrong."

Neve closed her eyes, picturing the girl once again. So serene, she had almost seemed resigned to death.

"'There are no keys for those handcuffs, not here,' Rick said. He pulled two things out of his jacket: a small pocket knife, and a pistol. I don't know much about guns, I don't know what kind it was. He pointed it at the ceiling, and pulled the trigger. The hole wasn't too small, and I thought I was the next target. Aimed at somebody's face, I don't think there'd be much left. That's when I started praying again.

"I hadn't prayed," Neve said, "hadn't been to church at all, since I was a girl.

"He gave me the gun. 'Kill me,' he said. 'Stop me from sinning again. You're my avenging angel, my only hope. Save me, and save her. Or sacrifice us both. Either way, you're free to leave.' He turned to the girl, played with the knife in his hand, and added over his shoulder, 'Remember, though, if I don't die tonight, I do know where you live.'"

Neve shuddered. As if the ghost weren't enough, and the possibility of a demon, there was a true, natural psychotic who had her address. She sighed. He could return at any time; she'd practically forgotten that with everything else. She couldn't go to the police. She knew nothing about him, except the location of the warehouse which was probably owned under a false name, no less real than Rick. So the first thing the police might learn would be that someone had murdered their informant, Neve Spirito, in her apartment.

"I should have shot him. He played with the girl a while, waiting I guess for me to shoot him. He wanted me to, but I couldn't. I just couldn't." She hugged herself. "I couldn't just kill him. I dropped the gun and ran. I ran out of the bedroom. Rick followed, laughing. He told me where the door was. It was unlocked, and I left that warehouse. I've never gone back.

"There were shelves storing the rings he collected. I didn't know if he actually planned to kill the girl. I hoped it was all a prank someone played on me. A sick, perverted prank, but nothing more. I never believed that." Neve turned to the gargoyle; he hadn't moved since she began the story, and stared intently at her. "She came to me, that girl, as a ghost. She came that night. And I could have saved her."

Footsteps approached. Father O'Leary came through the door onto the altar. "Dinner waits," he said. He looked at the gargoyle. "I don't suppose you eat."

The gargoyle shook his head and leaned close to Neve. "You can't undo what's been done," he whispered, "but you can do something about it. *We* can do something about it. The ghost wants justice? We can bring her justice. I have ordered it done to others, for lesser crimes. Lead me to this warehouse. I can wait for days, weeks, for him to return there. I can deliver justice."

Neve shook her head. Was that what it would take to get rid of the ghost? Was this justice? "You'd kill him? On my word alone?"

"I trust your word. Explicitly," the gargoyle said. "I hear your heart beat, I hear you breathe, and I recognize when a person lies. Either you tell me the truth, or you at least believe it to be true; either is more condemning than a story about a man wearing his best suit on the wrong day."

Neve looked at the priest, and then at the gargoyle. "In a way, he is a demon," the gargoyle added. "It's my function to rid the world of demons."

<hr />

"I can't ask you to kill him," Neve told the gargoyle.

He looked at her for a moment. In too many ways, she reminded him of Magdelina: a quality of innocence ran through her blood, though outwardly she denied it. Rick must have known this about her; he'd given her a choice between death and death. *Kill*, he had told her, *or I will.* And he did. Neither taking his life, nor leaving him to take the girl's life, would have been acceptable options to Neve Spirito. The gargoyle could not find her at fault.

"You didn't ask," the gargoyle told her. "Perhaps freeing the world of a man like Rick is exactly what I need to be admitted into heaven." Perhaps she was his angel, after all.

Father O'Leary stepped closer. He looked from the gargoyle to the woman, and then back to the gargoyle. "You intend to break His commandments. Thou shall not kill. God offers no interpretation which justifies murder."

"God kills," the gargoyle told him, "so it cannot be as simple as that. We all die, you and I and every man, woman, and child who has walked through these walls. God takes us all. Sometimes, He arranges for one of us to clean our own world. How many women has this man killed already? How many will he kill in the future, if I don't stop him now? I see it as one more life on my hands, or the blood of his countless, future victims. The choice, to me, is clear."

"It is not clear," the priest said.

"It's not your choice." The gargoyle turned again to Neve. "Would you show me this warehouse?"

"And if he's not there?" Neve asked.

"I'll wait."

He remembered the apparition, her pleading words: "There is no justice." The gargoyle had brought justice to his world once before, the day he ended his life. He intended to bring it again.

"You don't know that this would change anything," Father O'Leary told him.

"Everything has changed already," the gargoyle said. He brought his hands up before his face, admired them. "I move. I am animate. I am more than just a mere statue, and this is a new sensation. I preached God's word long enough to know the purpose of gargoyles in the church, and now I move to fulfill that role. These years that I watched, I sought demons. Perhaps there were demons among us, something worse than the creatures described in the Bible. Something closer to us. This Rick is no mere man. He collects the rings of women. He steals their innocence, steals their lives, and keeps souvenirs."

"I only saw the rings," Neve said, "and the one woman. I never saw him kill her."

"I saw her ghost," the gargoyle reminded her. "That is evidence enough. It carries far greater weight than the evidence I used to convict better men."

"Perhaps God gave you this stone body as a lesson," the priest said, "to learn that murder is not an answer."

The gargoyle extended his wings and leaned closer to Neve. "Are you going to lead me to this warehouse, or should I look for it on my own?"

"Tell me one thing," she said, lowering her head. "Do you think the ghost will leave me when he dies?"

The gargoyle drew his wings back, and frowned. "I don't know that."

How could they consider this?

Father O'Leary looked from Neve to the gargoyle as they spoke. His words meant nothing to them. Didn't the gargoyle realize that he'd been punished for murder? Even if the victim was not innocent, Father O'Leary couldn't justify murder. The gargoyle had once again assumed the role he'd played during his life: Judge, jury, and executioner. If he wanted to end this punishment, this life as a gargoyle, didn't he realize that committing the same sin now would only prolong his exile from heaven?

Father O'Leary couldn't listen anymore. "Think about this," he told Neve, "before you agree. Think over dinner, which is ready." He looked to the gargoyle and shook his head. "If you murder this man, you might find yourself trapped in that body for much longer."

"Perhaps," the gargoyle said, "but I don't look at it that way. This may be my chance for redemption. And if it's not, at least my conscious will have something clean to remember."

"If you consider murder a clean act," Father O'Leary said.

"As a prevention of more, yes," the gargoyle told him.

After the dinner crowd had gone, Angie took the extras out back. Some days, she had nothing left to give; others, like today, the deli did little business.

It did little business today because of the police. A half dozen bodies had been found at the warehouse across the street. They'd all been customers. Willie had been something more than just a customer.

No more. Now, he was a corpse, carved like the roast beef he so greatly loved.

She'd always given away the extras to the street. They seemed to love her for it, though any one of them might easily stick her if they thought she had a dollar to give. She worried about their drugs, too, whether it be the bottle or the needle. But she never dwelled on it; they needed food. And tonight, she needed diversion.

The usual small crowd gathered, with one noticeable exception. "Where's Gus?" Angie asked Penelope. She didn't know everyone by name, but these two and a few others were special to her. They'd been here from the beginning.

Penelope sighed, but didn't offer much of an answer. Gus had been ranting, recently, about angels. From the look on Penelope's face, Angie was sure he'd joined them.

The gargoyle waited as Neve dined with the priest. He pictured, too vividly, the Rick of Neve's story walking into his warehouse to find a stone statue in the darkness.

The gargoyle stood guard over the church, above the double doors which led into the street. He could leave, but had no desire to go while his angel was two rooms away. It was for her, and perhaps for Magdelina as well, that he wanted to punish Rick. The man had exploited Neve's inability to kill. But when the choice was kill or allow another to die, and there really was no choice but death, Neve Spirito couldn't actively choose to kill. So instead, she'd left, and passively chose the girl's death. Which guilt, the gargoyle wondered, was worse to live with?

And as Rick had taken advantage of Neve, so the gargoyle had done the same to his Magdelina. The only variation was that he had chosen Magdelina's death. She had no option at all, not even a clue that something was to happen. He had sealed Magdelina's fate without even an explanation.

He wanted to go back and reverse his decision. He wanted to take his life before hers, rather than after. She'd had a life to live, a child to raise. Without consideration, he'd punished the girl in stealing her mother, in having her watch her mother burn.

What became of that girl? Obviously, she'd lived to have children of her own or her blood couldn't have flowed today through the veins of Neve Spirito. Nothing confirmed this belief but the silky snow hair and those eyes. They were too blue, like a clear sky just before sunset. They were the eyes of his beloved Magdelina, and so he loved Neve just for those eyes.

But again, the gargoyle's thoughts drifted to his child. She had been too young to survive on her own; someone must have taken her in. She may have lived on the streets as a common prostitute for years. Her child might have been born in one of those illicit unions, and even that child's child. How many generations did Magdelina's children struggle to break away from the less savory city streets and into what Neve Spirito had become?

What, exactly, was Neve Spirito? Independent, she was not invulnerable. She was wealthy enough to live in a large, spacious apartment, when many people in this city crowded into windowless rooms reminiscent of chambers reserved for the less fortunate guests of the Inquisition. Neve was an angel who painted angels, and she carried his blood.

Perhaps his purpose in this stone body was not to protect the church, but to protect his descendants. There might be others. Five hundreds years was a long time; if one person had only two children, and twenty years later they each have two children...he didn't try to complete the calculation. The number of his children on this earth could well be in the thousands, too high for the gargoyle to count.

In the rectory, Neve Spirito and Father O'Leary ate outside the gargoyle's range of hearing. He remembered food, though not the names of dishes or their tastes. He smelled nothing, tasted nothing.

Eventually, Father O'Leary led Neve back into the church.

There had been no visitors, so the gargoyle left his perch and landed in front of the altar.

Neve looked shyly at the gargoyle, like a girl might glance at a man she found interesting. "We don't have to do it now," the gargoyle told her.

"There are other ways to go about it, like I said," Father O'Leary told her. "Police. FBI. There are people trained to deal with men like Rick. You don't have to get any more involved than you are."

"And yet," she said, "how much more involved can I get? The girl comes to me, begs me to give her some form of justice, and the only thing I can think is that if I tell anyone, like the police, he'll find and kill me, too. Before they do anything to him, he'd make sure I joined her. I can't live with that fear." She shook her head and turned to the gargoyle. "I think we should leave."

The priest bowed his head. "I'll pray for you both to come back," he said. "Physically, and spiritually."

CHAPTER NINE

Chloe stared at him like he was a demon direct from hell, which of course he was. But she didn't know that. She actually responded quite well; he thought she'd be afraid of him. He thought her act would fall apart when faced with reality. Wrong, he smiled.

"Close the door," Rick said. She did so, without a word, without tearing her eyes from him for one second.

He had the lights out. He saw darkness; where there was less light, he saw more clearly. Dad had mentioned this photosensitivity, saying it would pass. Presently, Rick wanted it as dark as possible. Blankets hung over the two kitchen windows, to prevent light from getting in.

"He wasn't a vampire," Rick told her. "I know you thought he was, but I don't know that there is such a thing. He was so scared, he shit his pants before I touched him. Do you think your vampire would do something like that?"

He no longer felt his own fear; there had been a time, not too long ago, when he'd tried to prevent what was happening. He had found his angel at an art show, a timid woman who had painted a wonderful angel. She had seemed to be the perfect choice for savior; there was something pure about her, about the way her hair was the color of snow and her eyes the color of the sky. He liked her smile and the way she met his eyes.

Looking back, he realized he'd chosen her

specifically because she wouldn't be able to pull the trigger. Subconsciously, he didn't want to die; or, at least, the thing which grew within him refused to die. But there was no *thing*, in fact; it was just an aspect of himself.

Almost fully realized now, that thing he called demon had a strong enough sense of self-preservation to pick an angel who couldn't succeed, a woman whose paintings revealed something of what was inside her, something pure and innocent and untouched by evil.

He'd looked into her life, studied everything he could find: Neve Spirito, a graphic designer for an advertising agency, though she could have been so much more if she'd wanted it. Her parents had died when she was young, leaving her an inheritance and no need for a job. She worked because, though the art was part of her, she couldn't trust her life to it. She worked in the corporate world not because she had to, but because she was afraid not to. It was strange, the way she wanted nothing more than to do her own art and worked instead on the projects for others whose only interests were money. This, and more, he'd learned through casual conversation with a pretty woman from Neve's office; her fingers had been, unfortunately, bare.

In a way, Chloe was similar to his angel Neve: whereas Chloe thought she wanted something and didn't know how to pursue it, his angel knew she wanted something and didn't trust herself to pursue it.

Chloe came closer, slowly, bringing him out of his thoughts. "What are you, then?" She had completely forgotten the man at the party.

He laughed, but gave no answer. He wasn't sure what to do with her; if she carried his seed, he'd have no second child, so she needed his protection. Some people were sensitive to what she carried; given an opportunity, they'd do anything to prevent Rick's child from being born, even if it meant their lives and their souls.

Rick knew little about souls. That people had them, he had no doubt; his father had raised him Catholic, mostly, and what many Catholics believed, Rick also believed in: the Father, the Son, the Holy Spirit, life everlasting. He believed Jesus descended into hell and then ascended into heaven. The saints were fools, sacrificing their mortal lives to achieve greatness in another world they knew nothing about. The most unforgivable sin was to be untrue to oneself. His nature was like that of his father, and his father, and a hundred generations of fathers before that. His was the nature of The Beast. His was the mission of vengeance upon the world; when he found sinners who didn't deserve life, he took it from them. He based his judgments on observation, like his father before him. The people at the party, giving their lives to drugs and sex and other foolishness, perhaps deserved the greater punishment of living their wasted lives. But since the change was not complete in Rick, the urge to destroy was stronger than the need for control. The little party had been an excellent first adventure.

Rick flexed his fingers; he wanted to take demonic

form again. He wanted to rip more lives from the night, send them down to hell where they belonged.

Instead, he stood. "We're going out," he told Chloe, tossing her the car keys. "I'll tell you how to get there."

She touched his chest and lips and whispered, "I'd rather stay here, try that baby thing again."

He slapped her, throwing her into the door. It shuddered when she crashed into it. He would learn control, especially when it came to Chloe. Soon, she wouldn't need to be controlled. She'd lay, like a good little girl, and wait for her time to come. When their child was finally born, her time would end. He smiled at the thought; if Chloe didn't carry his child, he could always find another, more suitable vessel.

⚓

Chloe pulled the car into the warehouse. Warm, comforting darkness greeted Rick's eyes. The garage closed automatically; Rick was out of the car before Chloe turned off the ignition.

"It's empty," she said, getting out of the car.

But it wasn't completely empty. There was the Trophy Room and there was the computer desk. He went to the desk and turned on the system. The hum of the computer replaced the eerie silence which he so thoroughly enjoyed. If he listened hard enough, he heard Chloe's heart racing. He heard her breathe. His senses—all his senses—were at their height, and he loved it.

He wanted someone other than Chloe; there was no room in his heart for love anymore, no room for caring. "This is where I go, sometimes," he told her.

"Here?" Chloe asked. She twirled, slowly, taking in the iron railings of the ceiling, the high fluorescent lights he never turned on. The walls were steel and chrome; the space of the warehouse had only one function: to overwhelm.

It was huge. Still in the midst of the change, Rick's wings hadn't yet grown out. When they did, when he was twice the size of a man, there was enough space for him to fly within these walls.

"My Trophy Room," he told Chloe.

"Not a whole lot of trophies."

He wanted to hit her, but held back. Though the car separated them, he could have easily vaulted over it and struck her with enough force to sever her head. He didn't need a demon's body to do that; she was too thin, too fragile. He doubted she could go full term with his child.

He curled both hands into fists and closed his eyes. "In there," he said, nodding toward the office. He wanted to hit her, rip her apart, but he couldn't hurt Chloe. He needed someone else to hurt. He needed to finish here first.

Chloe opened the office door. She found the light switch on the side of the wall; blazing, the lights burned Rick's eyes even through closed eyelids. *Temporary,* Dad had told him. He stepped toward the room. *Temporary, and harmless.*

Chloe stood at the doorway and stared at the huge white bed while her mouth hung open. She stared at the mirrors, and stepped closer, transfixed by her own images in them. She touched one of the gymnastic rings, caressed it with a finger.

Rick, calm and controlled, turned off the lights. He saw so much better in the dark. He looked immediately at the shelves which housed his collection of rings. The latest, an emerald cut diamond in a platinum setting, was the most valuable and fascinating. It was the ring he'd tried to stop himself with. It had been a foolish thing to do, giving a loaded gun to an *Angel of Mercy*. Fleeing, she'd confirmed that there were no angels. There was his Dad, and himself. There was a God who stood by and watched the world He had created crumble onto itself. But angels? Those were myth.

"I can't see," Chloe said. She controlled her fear surprisingly well.

"There's nothing more to see," he told her. "Go to the bed. Lie down."

She did so. He saw her as though the sun shined above at midday. She breathed more quickly, and he heard the rapid pounding of her heart. This excited her; her excitement nauseated Rick.

He moved to the bed, swiftly. He pushed her down when she tried to rise and meet him. She kissed at his chest as he pulled her toward the back of the bed. "Yes," she whispered, shedding what little clothing she wore.

He bound one of her wrists with the handcuffs.

"Cool," she breathed.

With some force, he pulled her other hand to a second cuff and clasped it tightly around her wrist. She purred beneath him, straining against the cuffs to touch him with her tongue. He slapped her, throwing her back down to the bed. "Stop," he said.

Rick proceeded to bind her legs. She was naked, writhing on the bed like a cat in heat. It sickened him. He smelled the excitement in her sweat. "I have someplace to go."

"What?" she asked. Rick climbed off the bed and walked toward the Trophy Room door. "What?" she repeated, louder.

He slammed the door shut behind her. She screamed his name. He left the car; he couldn't see well enough in the light—even in the light of midnight—to drive.

On the street, the moon hurt his eyes. The streetlights around his Brooklyn warehouse were all out; he'd shattered each whenever they were replaced, knowing very well what to expect.

He flexed his arms, felt the rippled muscles bulge against his flesh. He wanted, needed, to use them. His body changed beneath his clothes, and tore them completely as he grew. He didn't yet have control.

He looked down at his green fists. His color was still too sickly, not quite what it would be. He felt the fledgling wings on his back; he stretched them, flapped them once. They had no strength. Not yet.

He ran. Running expended energy, allowed him to let out some of his frustration. The anger, though, remained. Twenty minutes later, he stopped.

There was a bridge nearby. He looked to it, but knew better than to cross it as a demon. Secrecy was important. He should strike from the shadows, and retreat into the shadows with only a witness or two to ever say they had seen something other than a man. In this world, a few scattered stories would earn rubber rooms and tight white jackets for the tellers. If a hundred people saw him in the same place, he'd find a drawing of himself on the front page of *The Post*.

He walked away from the bridge, frantically extending and retracting his fingers. Anticipation frustrated Rick. The first person he spotted, drunk and completely without challenge, became his victim. Rick's claws tore through his chest like a sword through air; he tasted the blood that spilled from the man's body. Too much of that and he might get drunk himself.

The man was fortunate. He died so quickly, he had no time to feel the pain. Rick stood over the body and stared a moment at the gaping holes he'd gouged. A smile crept across Rick's face, and he moved on for a second, more substantial kill.

⚬——⚬

For the moment, Neve forgot where they were going. Their method of travel distracted her.

She sat on the gargoyle's back, above his wings — which didn't flap, but extended straight out like wings on an airplane — with her arms wrapped around his neck. He'd told her he felt nothing, neither her weight nor pressure on his throat as she clung to him.

Below them, the city was amazing. There were cars, too distant to see in detail but not so far away that they were just dots. Some buildings rose higher than they flew. They moved so quickly, few people were likely to clearly see them.

The city was like a three dimensional map. Stairs led down to subways. Buses stopped next to plexi-glass half-booths. Billboards looked up at her rather than down. Bums slept in alleys and college kids staggered to a party.

Neve rarely stayed up this late during her real life, but real life had ended with Rick's invitation to shoot him. She should have pulled the trigger and ended it then; his ghost would not have come back complaining that there was no justice. He'd asked for it. Begged for it. If she'd had more courage that day, enough to just shoot the killer and be done with it, she wasn't sure where she'd be today. She just knew it wasn't on top of the world, with a gargoyle as her seat and transportation and fist of justice.

Of course, on top of the world—that's the only place she could call it when she rode the gargoyle—was not such a bad place to be. But afraid to return to her apartment, unable to sleep, hallucinating demons—there may have been a lot of strange things in New York City's alleys, but green skinned demons were not among them—didn't do her much good. A psychiatrist would ask her to start at the beginning. She'd have to tell the story again, about Rick and the trigger she couldn't pull. Who would believe she'd flown across New York City on the back of a gargoyle? A non-practicing Catholic such as herself, granted a miracle by God? Even Father O'Leary wouldn't have believed if he hadn't actually seen it.

Neve found it difficult enough to believe herself. For all she knew, she still slept on a bench in Central Park. The bum who had called out to her might stand over her, watching, still calling her an angel. There had been too much of that. Neve knew one thing, and one thing only, about angels: she was not one.

"There," Neve said, pointing to the warehouse as it came into view. It was odd, that she recognized it from such a different vantage point. She knew it by instinct; it was in this place that life as she had known it had ended and the nightmare began. In this particular nightmare, the ghosts appeared when she opened her eyes.

Still, it startled her that she knew the place so easily. One night out of thousands which had passed through her life. Not even an hour. Yet she knew it like she would know home: she saw something of herself there, something she'd lost. Dignity? Sanity? It waited for her in that warehouse.

The gargoyle swooped down. No lights shone in its windows. Even the surrounding streetlights were all out, and some traffic signals cast no colors. A blackout, on a night which seemed perfectly average for everyone in the world but her? No. As they came closer, she saw broken glass on the street at some of the lights.

Someone had put them out.

Windows near the top of the warehouse, visible as they approached, faced all directions. They'd been painted black.

The gargoyle landed on the gravel floor of the warehouse's roof. A large metal structure with a single door stood in its center.

The gargoyle stooped to allow Neve off his back. "Wait here," he said. He went to the door. The handle resisted him; rather than argue with it, the gargoyle ripped the door completely free.

"So much for subtlety," Neve whispered. The gargoyle either didn't hear her—which she doubted—or ignored the comment as he entered the blackened stairway.

Neve wondered, not for the first time, if this was the right path. But now, at least, there was no turning back, no second guessing herself. She'd chosen a course of action, to guide the gargoyle to this warehouse, and had followed through with it.

The rest was, she realized, out of her hands. Just like the girl's life when she fled.

Dark meant little to the gargoyle.

He descended the metal staircase quickly. He didn't step on the stairs; they appeared too feeble to hold him. Instead, he drifted above them.

The stairs spiraled down the full length of the warehouse. It was empty, as Neve had described it. Electronic equipment sat on a lonely desk. There was an automobile near the garage door. The office, set apart from the rest of the warehouse, had no ceiling of its own. It housed a large bed and mirrors and shelves full of rings. The slow, steady breathing the gargoyle heard belonged to a girl on the bed. She lay there, pale, handcuffed, with her eyes closed and her head tilted to one side. But she did not sleep.

The gargoyle landed softly at the foot of the bed. "Rick!" the girl cried, hopeful, anxious.

"No," the gargoyle said. He wanted to wrap his stone hands around Rick's neck and take him on a flight over the ocean. Presently, though, the man was gone and the girl was more important. Handcuffs held both her arms and legs to the bed.

"How long have you been here?" he asked.

"Are you looking for Rick?"

"I am," the gargoyle said. "I'm going to free you now."

"Oh." She showed no excitement at being released.

The gargoyle grabbed the hoop of the cuff attached to the bed and crushed it. The three other cuffs, on her legs and other arm, broke just as easily. The girl sat up. Her clothes littered the floor, but she made no effort to dress.

"You can go now," the gargoyle told her. She nodded, but nothing more. The gargoyle lifted a discarded jacket from the floor and offered it to her. She took it, held it, but didn't put it on.

"You're not a vampire," the girl said, disappointed. "What are you?"

"That's not important," the gargoyle told her.

"I guess not."

The girl stared blankly at him. She looked sick, thin, and pale. But her heart had a strong, healthy beat. She breathed regularly. Still, she didn't move.

"Are you okay?" he asked. "Can you walk?"

"No," she said. "I don't feel well at all."

"Get dressed," the gargoyle told her. "We'll get you help." He left the office and quickly scanned the warehouse. He saw nothing different, heard no sound. He flew to the ceiling, around the staircase, and out onto the roof.

Neve stood with her arms crossed before her chest. She stared, not at him, but at something to his left.

He looked over. The ghost stood there. "There is no justice," it said.

"There will be," he told it.

The apparition faded. The gargoyle stepped forward and told Neve, "There's a girl downstairs. Take her to a healer. There's an automobile. I'll wait here for Rick to return."

"He's not here?" Neve asked.

"No." *But he will be.* And he'd find a gargoyle waiting for him.

The gargoyle hung upside down from the ceiling by grasping one of the metal beams with his feet. His wings extended outwards. The moment Rick returned, silence would cloak the gargoyle as he launched.

The car was gone. Rick would see that immediately, but he might think the girl had found a way to escape on her own. He would be wary, possibly expecting some form of retaliation, but there was no way he'd be prepared for what waited for him. He'd never expect it to come from above.

In those final moments of life, Rick would see only one thing: the grotesque stone face of the gargoyle. He would feel only stone hands as they crushed his life. He would only hear his own screams.

The gargoyle was eager to complete this. He didn't relish the thought of taking another life; but destroying this man—a demon among men if ever one walked the earth—would save lives. The girl was only the first. Neve, too, for surely Rick would eventually seek her out and finish what he'd started.

The silence of the warehouse was complete. Little noise penetrated the thick walls. Some sounds did come through the broken door on the roof, but there were few sounds in this part of the city. The streets were deserted, as though people, and even the block itself, knew what went on within these walls. Each of the forty-three rings on that shelf represented a victim. One of those rings had belonged to the ghost which haunted Neve now. None belonged here.

Someone, seeing the gargoyle, might think this living statue to be a monster. Perhaps during life, they thought of him the same way. But his life was over. He couldn't reverse the things he'd done, but he could attempt to set things in balance. By removing Rick from the world, he might not save as many lives as he'd taken, but it was a beginning.

There was a sound: a key inserted into the lock of a door. A door, next to the garage door Neve had used to take the car out, swung open. Very little light filtered in from behind the man as he entered.

Rick!

The gargoyle took everything about him in a glance: short, dark hair, muscular, very well-built—for a man. But the gargoyle was no mere man, and no matter how strong Rick was, he wasn't as strong as stone. Rick walked with an arrogant confidence, blanketed by the belief that nothing could touch him.

He was wrong.

Rick stopped, suddenly, and stared at the spot the car had occupied. The keys had still been in the girl's clothes, but the gargoyle really didn't care what the man thought.

The gargoyle tightened his fists. Below, Rick did the same.

Rick sprinted to the office with the bed and the rings. He moved faster than any other man. He threw the office door open with so much force, he tore it from its hinges.

The gargoyle released the metal beam and descended. There was a slight sound, a reverberation. It should have been nothing, or close enough to nothing to be unimportant. Still, the man spun immediately toward the gargoyle.

The eyes which stared up at the gargoyle glowed red. It was almost enough stop him.

He landed next to the man. Rick stood taller than the gargoyle. His chest was broader, his arms hugely muscular. His clothes, already torn, shredded as the man's body expanded. The transformation ended in seconds, and Rick stood a foot taller than the gargoyle.

"You," Rick—the demon—said, an accusation filled with recognition. Its eyes were a luminous red, its skin a greenish brown. Wings hid behind its back. Its hands were claws, its teeth jagged and stained with blood. It lunged forward, throwing all its weight and muscle against the stone body of the gargoyle.

Rick's attack threw the gargoyle a dozen yards across the floor of the warehouse, taking him completely off his feet. Before the gargoyle could react, Rick—the demon—threw itself at him again. It landed on top of the gargoyle, straddled him, and wrestled both his hands to the ground.

An inch separated their faces. The demon's saliva dripped, unfelt, onto the gargoyle. It bared its teeth, and lifted an arm to strike again, freeing one of the gargoyle's arms.

The gargoyle swung his freed arm at the demon's head. With a satisfying crack, he threw the creature off.

The gargoyle jumped to his feet, just as the demon picked itself up.

The gargoyle looked at his hand. Demon blood dirtied it, but there was no feeling: no pain, no pressure, no shock of the assault. The gargoyle smiled. His was a solid, stone body, sculpted over a century ago. The demon had a body of flesh and of blood.

The demon shook itself and touched the side of its head where blood seeped out. Unlike the gargoyle, it apparently felt pain.

The gargoyle flew toward the demon, striking the creature in its chest and throwing it against the wall. The office shook. Inside, rings clattered from their shelves by the vibration like a rain of gold over the sound of the demon's heart and labored breathing. *Labored* breathing; the demon was hurt.

The demon struck swiftly, swinging claws with full force. It scraped the gargoyle's body with a loud, painful sound. The sound hurt the gargoyle's ears, but there was no real pain. There was no blood. Only fury.

The gargoyle punched the demon. It staggered. The gargoyle swung again. The demon fell backwards, avoiding the arm.

"You can't exist," the demon whispered as he retreated into the shadows.

"Neither can you," the gargoyle said. He flew forward again. He raised both feet and kicked Rick. Something in the demon snapped, maybe bones; Rick fell through the wall of the office and shattered the wooden bed frame as he landed on it. Greenish-red blood spilled on the sheets. There would be no more victims in this bed.

The gargoyle grabbed Rick by the neck and rose into the air. The demon's wings fluttered uselessly, without strength; it tried to pull free, but had no leverage.

The gargoyle carried it into the air. He reveled in this test of his strength; without a sense of touch, he could fight this demon for a century without feeling pain or fatigue.

The demon struggled as they ascended. Perhaps there were no limits to the gargoyle's strength; he was stone, not flesh and blood. He had no muscles to build, only a thick rock skeleton. He tightened his fingers around the demon's throat and listened as Rick struggled to inhale.

"I called you demon," the gargoyle told it, "but I never imagined it was true. Now I see why the gargoyle is such a strong defender against demons. You have no strength, next to the earth's stone." Near the ceiling, he released the demon. Rick fell twenty yards. The concrete floor cracked when he landed.

The gargoyle looked down at the demon. It was confused, struggling to stand but apparently unsure of which way was up. It pushed from the floor, and looked up at the gargoyle. Its red eyes flickered, dimly, and something of fear covered its face.

The gargoyle knew the look of fear better than any man alive. He'd chiseled fear onto the faces of the condemned; it had plastered the faces of men and women who never knew their crime, not even when serving their punishment. Fire brought fear to the eyes of the strongest men. It was this look, the moment before death was accepted, that the gargoyle found on the demon's face.

That brief reminiscence was all the demon needed. On its feet again, Rick ran out the door of the warehouse.

The gargoyle flew through the windows set near the ceiling, sending shards of blackened glass to the street below. He found the demon easily. The alleys were too narrow to hide something with the demon's bulk. It ran with a limp and spilled a trail of discolored blood.

Unable to think straight, Rick fled the warehouse. He hadn't thought very well since the change began, but now he couldn't even focus his eyes or stand upright. His head ached. Blood seeped from his torn flesh. It healed, too, but how quickly could he heal with the gargoyle continually beating on him?

He remembered, very well, the first time he'd seen the gargoyle. It stood above the double doors of the church. Dad had pointed to it. "That statue is alive. He doesn't know it himself, but it's his job, his mission, to protect the church from demons." It was their own little private joke. The gargoyle had stared at the whole congregation, never aware of the demons attending his church.

Yet here it was, that very same gargoyle, in Rick's warehouse.

The Trophy Room had been destroyed. There was no point trying to convince himself otherwise. He wanted another trophy, the head of a defeated gargoyle, but he lacked the strength.

His body tried to revert to human form. He resisted; one punch from the gargoyle would shatter his life. He couldn't die now. He was only just beginning. All that came before was a game, in preparation for the day he changed. Now that day was upon him, and this gargoyle intended to end it prematurely.

Rick didn't look back. He ran, crashing into the brick walls of the warehouse and the adjoining building several times. The alley was narrow, too narrow. There was no place to hide. He couldn't run quickly enough. He felt the gargoyle above him, following with its eyes before attacking again.

Dad would know what to do. Dad had seen things. Dad knew the gargoyle lived; had he sent it as a test? Rick clenched his fists and ran harder. Dad wouldn't do something like that to his only child, would he? No, because there would be no others. Unless Rick fathered a son, they would cease to exist.

No, something else, someone else, was responsible. Only one person, other than his father, had ever walked away from the warehouse: the white-haired Angel of Mercy who had failed him. Maybe she hadn't failed after all?

But it was too late! The change was mostly done; he

had no more doubts about his place in the world. He existed to destroy sinners. All were stained with Original Sin at birth, so no one was undeserving of Rick's judgment. Even the gargoyle, surely, must deserve death; but how did he kill stone?

The gargoyle swooped down at him. Rick stumbled sideways, almost falling. The gargoyle missed. The statue moved faster. It had full use of its wings. Every advantage, even surprise, belonged to it.

"Not fair," Rick mumbled, but he didn't stop to argue with God or Fate. He turned down another alley and ran faster. He had to escape and knew only one place the gargoyle might not be able to follow.

The gargoyle swept at him again, smashing him in the back of the head. Rick flew forward two dozen feet, skidding across pavement until he emerged from the alley. On the street, one car smashed another. They were the only two cars moving, but Rick didn't care. He pushed through them; it took every ounce of strength to push the Cadillac away from the sewage cover. The gargoyle swung down again, but not before Rick tore the cover free. He allowed his body to revert back to human and slipped into the tiny sewage hole. He fell through the darkness and splashed into sewage. The disgusting liquid moved swiftly, carrying him away from his warehouse and his Trophy Room.

If the gargoyle pursued, he didn't hear it. Rick listened to his body begin the painful process of repairing itself.

The gargoyle rose above the street; below, the demon slid through a manhole and disappeared, leaving two drivers awestruck. Two was not a large number. They may never tell anyone what they'd seen. The secret of the demon should be safe.

It was not safe from the gargoyle, though. He had seen the creature in both human and demonic form. He needed no rest, and would devote all his time to purging that beast from the world.

This was the demon Neve had seen, obviously, the creature which watched her from the alley. If the demon watched Neve, he knew she'd come to St. Lazarus'. Rick not only knew where the gargoyle resided, but who had sent him.

The gargoyle couldn't follow the demon into the sewers; the hole was too small. Strong as he was, he didn't think he could break through the asphalt. He didn't want to try. But Neve Spirito was not safe. She wouldn't be safe until the demon was found and destroyed.

He flew toward the cathedral. Eventually, Neve would return. If the demon tracked her by scent, it probably already stalked her. If for no reason other than revenge, the demon wanted her dead. The gun Rick had given Neve might have been useless, only a game.

The demon had moved with inhuman speed and agility. Its strength at least matched the gargoyle's. But the gargoyle felt none of Rick's attacks; therefore, the advantage was his. He looked at his arms, at the demon's blood. He had no blood of his own, no flesh to pierce. He was stone.

He didn't know how much pain or damage the demon could endure. It had taken a severe beating, yet managed to escape, albeit crooked and slowly. But the gargoyle couldn't count on him being wounded when they met again; if the demon was supernatural, he might be invulnerable, or at least, a fast healer. Maybe if the gargoyle learned the demon's true name, and therefore his home, he would have an additional advantage.

CHAPTER TEN

Gus woke in the middle of the alley. No sun. The kid lay next to him, bloody and torn. The blood was dry now, on the kid and the street, and Gus as well. He stared at his hands. Clean of blood, his fists hadn't killed the kid.

He couldn't trust what he'd seen before blacking out. A creature? One eye still saw nothing but red. What kind of creature would spare him?

Some creature had spared him. The kid was as dead as he'd intended Gus to be. One of *them*, but who had stopped him? Why? Had the Hand of God come down to wipe His earth clean? Were there others, like this kid, fallen all across the city and the world? The priest had said the stone angel would fly again; maybe the angel had come and lent Gus his strength.

Whatever the reason, the kid was dead on the ground. Flies were everywhere. And rats: the creatures of hell, come forth to claim one of their own. They could all rot in hell, even the kids. Where were morals in this world? Where was Jesus in the lives of man?

Gus stumbled down the alley. His vision was severely blurred, almost crooked, and everything had a scarlet tint. His legs didn't work properly, but that might have been fear or shock. Waking up after that was a thousand times worse than any hangover. At least when he drank, he knew the pain would subside.

Maybe it wasn't an angel, but a devil, which had

stopped the kid. Gus never had an easy life. It would be rougher if these wounds were permanent. If his vision never cleared, he might not see *them* approach until *they* were already on top of him!

And the things he saw, they were different now. He paid no attention to that. Now wasn't the time.

Jesus, and the saints, will march over *them*. God had sent his angels; one stone, another protecting Gus. He felt the goodness in the air around him; the angel watched over him still. Watched, guided, and protected. Yes, Gus needed protection, because *they* were everywhere and showed no sign of relenting.

On the street, Gus met the frightened eyes of strangers. There was nothing unusual about this. Always, he was looked at with something between contempt and fear. Often, one overshadowed the other. Tonight, terror reigned supreme. Something else was there, too, something Gus ignored.

A child pointed at Gus, and the mother swatted his arm. Gus ignored the pair, because she was going to die in seven years and the child was going to jump from crime to crime until finally getting killed—but these were things Gus shouldn't have known.

He didn't know where he was or where he was going. He knew only that *they* watched him. *They* could watch until God came down and eradicated *them*, because angels guarded Gus now. Nothing could harm him.

Neve Spirito ran into the church. Father O'Leary sat in the front pew with an open Bible. He turned when the doors opened and smiled sadly at her.

"Was he there?" the priest asked.

Neve stopped running, halfway between the doors and the altar. She gasped for breath and stared at the peaceful, quiet priest. "No," she said between breaths, "but there was a girl."

A surprised expression crossed the priest's face, quickly replaced by sadness. "Alive?"

"Yes, alive," Neve said, walking the final half of the aisle. "I took her to a hospital." She hated hospitals. That's why she'd been running. She hated the thought of the woman, the hooker, with her stomach ripped open and bleeding, who had been brought in while Neve was there. Neve had looked at the woman's hair, the make-up, all of which had been streaked with blood. She'd left the girl. She had no intention to return.

"Good," the priest said, standing. "And the gargoyle?"

"Waiting for him about two hours now," Neve said. "You still think it's wrong? For him to wait, I mean?"

Father O'Leary shook his head. "It doesn't matter what I think. What do you think? Jesus tells us judgment awaits in heaven. Who are we to judge the actions of a man, when Jesus Christ said that only those without sin are fit to judge? The Lord's works are mysterious, not for our minds to comprehend.

"Yet, I have no heart to stop the gargoyle, because I believe this man is a monster." He looked down at the

Bible in his hands. "I couldn't find the right passage to tell me how to think. I can easily find the passage in Exodus in which our Lord commands that we shall not kill. But to prevent this man from committing this crime countless times, must we, too, kill? I find no justification for either action or inaction, my child. I find no consolation in the Word of the Lord."

The doors opened. The gargoyle entered. Neve immediately saw the blood on the gargoyle's arms.

Father O'Leary put down his Bible. The sound of the leather binding on the wooden pew echoed through the darkness of the church. Neve closed her eyes, though only for a moment. Should she be thankful? Would she be able to sleep now? "You found him," she said. "He's dead."

"He's not dead," the gargoyle said.

"Did you find forgiveness for this man, this monster?" Father O'Leary asked.

"Monster," the gargoyle repeated. "Your description is more accurate than you imagine." He stopped in front of Neve, leaned down and forward to look straight into her eyes. She saw nothing; they were stone. His rock countenance seemed incapable of more than just the most basic of expressions. "Neve, the demon you saw, in the alley: he and Rick are one and the same."

Neve's mouth dropped. Behind her, the priest sat heavily on the pew. In a way, it was a relief to know she hadn't imagined it.

After a moment of silence, Father O'Leary said, "Then you have vanquished your demon."

"I have *found* my demon," the gargoyle told him. "I have found a creature which legend says I must protect you, this whole church, from. Vanquished? Defeated? No, I can't say that. Not only have I not destroyed the demon, he most certainly knows the reason I came for him." He looked again at Neve. "I fear that, until he is dead, your life is in danger."

"If he knows I led you to him," Neve said, "then doesn't he know where we are now?"

The gargoyle nodded. "We need to find someplace safer for you," he said. "And you, too, Father O'Leary. He recognized me, which means he's been to St. Lazarus' before."

Father O'Leary looked down at his Bible. Neve watched him as he stood there, staring at the Book until, finally, he spoke. "This is holy ground, Gargoyle. Consecrated ground. No demon can enter the House of The Lord."

"I said," the gargoyle repeated, "he has already been here. There's no other way he could have recognized me."

"But there is," Father O'Leary said. "Remember the man who hoped to see his stone angel fly? How could you believe there were no other witnesses to your flight?" He shook his head. "God's house is the only sanctuary I will provide myself with. You are both welcome to stay. It's been your home, Gargoyle, far longer than it's been mine. You said yourself, you have never seen a demon in our church."

"I'll stay, too," Neve said. "If he comes here looking for me, you can end it here. I don't care where it ends, so long as it ends. I want to sleep again. I refuse to live in fear."

———

Rick staggered through his apartment and into bed. He fell, face down, and cried. The pain had subsided, the wounds were already more than half healed; he cried, instead, because there was nothing else he could do. His imagination conjured no way to defeat a statue. It had taken his strongest punches and laughed!

Rick never thought humiliation would accompany the change. He hated himself more than before, and hated his father. His mother, too; she should have died before giving birth, should have killed herself and the fetus that became Rick. Just as Chloe knew what Rick was, surely his mother had known Dad to be something more than human. Or less than human. Something other than human, at least.

Rick flipped onto his back and stared at the ceiling. He saw nothing but the gargoyle sweeping down at him, with wings that worked, with strength equal to his own.

Equal now, perhaps, but not when the change was done. Rick had achieved only a fraction of his future. The things he would know, the things he would accomplish, far outweighed what he'd ever done before.

But could he kill stone?

He was afraid that he might shatter the gargoyle

only to find each shard of stone alive and pursuing him. Had his choice of angel been better than he'd believed? Too late, bitch! He wanted to find her, hurt her, but the gargoyle would be there to protect her. How could he not expect Rick to seek revenge?

They would be at St. Lazarus'. Rick could arrive any time of day or night and find them inside that cathedral. They knelt before the altar and prayed to God for guidance against the evil which walked the earth. Though God couldn't—or, at least, wouldn't—help the woman; the gargoyle would. But their logic was flawed: God had created Rick to cleanse the earth; he was no demon.

He smashed his fists down on the bed, hard enough to put them through the mattress. How did a man destroy stone? He couldn't burn it, but did stone melt? Could Rick shatter it? Could he immobilize or imprison it? He reached for the phone, touched a speed dial number he never used, and listened as the phone rang. Twice. Three times, and the machine answered. "I need help," Rick said into the phone.

His father interrupted the machine on the other end. "You're changing," he said. "I told you what to expect."

"You told me," Rick agreed. "You told me about the gargoyle at the church, too. You knew it would come after me, didn't you? Did you send it, Dad? Did you send that thing after me?"

His father's next words were whispers. "Tell me what happened."

CHAPTER ELEVEN

Rick climbed the stairs of St. Lazarus' Cathedral. He stopped at the door and inhaled deeply. Inside, the gargoyle waited for him with Rick's failed angel. He looked forward to confronting the gargoyle again; stone did break, and he would break it.

He carried a bag over his shoulder. It held the tools with which he would destroy the gargoyle: two heavy sledge hammers, stolen from the window of a hardware store; a crowbar; half a dozen railroad spikes; and a pickaxe tied loosely to the top. Just as flesh bled, stone shattered; if Rick's talons weren't sharp enough—and they may not be, since the change wasn't yet complete—these weapons would be.

Dad had suggested the weapons, but otherwise offered nothing. "Fight your own battles, son. I've already fought most of mine." What had Rick expected, anyhow? After the change was done, after the gargoyle was broken and the angel dead, Rick would take care of both loose ends in his life. *Daddy* would die; the son always destroyed the father. And Chloe: she would lay very still for the next nine months. If her belly didn't begin growing, he'd open her up and find another to mother his child. She'd been a poor choice.

Rick inhaled deeply and kicked the door open. He hoped to tear it from its hinges, but apparently he wasn't that strong yet. He shoved his way through as the door bounced back. Though it cracked loudly, it didn't break. The gargoyle stood in the center of the aisle, five feet from the altar. The failed angel and a priest flanked him. The three turned as one to face the demon in their doorway. The humans were surprised; they'd never seen a demon before. The gargoyle, however, reacted immediately.

The statue flew toward him. Rick took the pick from the top of the bag; its end was a curved head, both edges sharp. He rushed forward to meet the gargoyle. As the change continued, his speed and strength increased, and even the healing process—which had completed itself in little more than an hour—hadn't slowed the change. He swung the axe; the gargoyle swung its stony claws.

At the last instant, Rick jumped to the side. The gargoyle missed, but he didn't. He struck exactly where he aimed, burying the axe deep in the statue's chest.

Rick grabbed a sledge hammer and leapt on the gargoyle's back. Before it reacted, he swung down, full strength, on the gargoyle's head.

The gargoyle reached over its head and grabbed Rick with both hands. It pulled, hard, wrenching Rick from its back and throwing him into the doors.

Rick returned to his feet instantly. He allowed himself a quick smile. There was a crack on the gargoyle's head, and the axe protruded from its chest. Though the damage was not enough to destroy the thing, it encouraged Rick. The smile faded quickly, though, when he realized the gargoyle stood between him and his bag of tricks.

The gargoyle pulled at the axe, yanked a second and a third time before it came loose, taking a chip out of the gargoyle's chest with it. Rick smiled again. If he had to smash the gargoyle into a thousand of those tiny chips, he would.

The gargoyle tightened his fist around the wooden handle of the axe until it splintered. It looked down at the hole in his chest, and again at Rick.

Rick swallowed hard; could a statue actually look mad? "You can break," he told the gargoyle.

It rushed toward him. Rick threw himself forward, and down. He tucked his head and rolled into the gargoyle's legs as it ran; toppling the statue. Rather than fall, it rose into the air on its wings.

Rick rolled until he reached his bag. On his knees, he reached into the canvas as the gargoyle came at him again. He hated that; why did the gargoyle fly when his own wings didn't yet work?

Didn't matter. When the sun set tomorrow night, Rick would fly and the gargoyle would be nothing but a pile of pebbles. He took two spikes and braced himself for the gargoyle's next attack.

<hr />

Neve didn't want to watch, but she couldn't keep her eyes off the fight. The gargoyle rose into the air, circled twice, and struck.

The demon appeared different, now, than it had in either her dream or the alley. She didn't recognize, or even focus, on those differences; the shadows had tricked her.

It was hard to believe this creature was the same man who had given her a gun and begged her to shoot. He was taller, broader, darker. His skin was something between green and brown, and his eyes had that red glow Neve remembered from the alley.

The gargoyle swung a fist and the demon thrust with two long spikes.

She closed her eyes; Neve was afraid the gargoyle would be hurt because of her. First the girl, now the gargoyle. Since her life became a nightmare, she'd brought pain to everyone.

She couldn't think of the demon as a man. She couldn't keep a name attached to it. She glanced instead at the priest. He stared silently at the battle, clutching the Bible tightly against his chest with both hands.

The gargoyle swung his fists at the demon, one then the other, continually. The demon thrust with the spikes, chipping the gargoyle's shoulder again and again.

The demon moved to avoid the punches, but couldn't escape them all. Blood sprayed with every connection. Neve breathed in short and rapid gasps, as though she were in the middle of the fight.

The demon jumped backwards, shattering the ends of two rows of pews. The gargoyle moved after it. The demon ducked under his punch, swinging an arm as it moved forward. The demon hit the gargoyle in the back and threw him into the pews.

From its bag, the demon withdrew another sledge hammer. He threw himself at the gargoyle, swinging hard.

This time, the gargoyle ducked. The hammer missed, and the momentum pulled the demon to the side.

Neve's stomach flipped as she watched. She gripped the back of a pew so tightly, her knuckles whitened even as her fingers slipped in sweat.

The gargoyle swung with both fists, hitting the demon in the head and the ribs. It dropped the sledge hammer and fell to its knees.

Father O'Leary prayed under his breath; Neve couldn't hear the words, but she understood the tone. She added her own, silent prayer.

The gargoyle rose into the air and kicked the demon with both legs. The demon slid toward the back wall of the church, away from Neve Spirito and Father O'Leary. No matter how many holes the demon chipped from his body, the gargoyle knew he couldn't fail. In the war against demons, God's grace laid on his side.

He flew high into the cathedral. The demon sprawled on the floor, struggling to stand. Its weapons were scattered. It breathed heavily, erratically. It bled severely from the head, chest, and ribs. The demon's weapons had cracked the gargoyle's stone body; the gargoyle, in response, had cracked the demon's bones.

He flew down, fast, and hit the demon squarely in the back. A loud snap echoed beneath St. Lazarus' ceilings.

The demon no longer attempted to escape. Instead, it struggled just to keep its eyes open. It moved its mouth, but only blood came out. It offered no more fight, only flailed its arms spasmodically.

The gargoyle heard Father O'Leary alternate between the Lord's Prayer and the Hail Mary. He'd gone through them each at least twice since the demon entered the church.

He heard Neve's heart racing at twice its normal speed.

He bent his head closer to the demon. It no longer held the shape of a demon. The twisted, shattered body beneath the gargoyle was human. It didn't breathe. Its heart no longer beat.

The gargoyle stepped off the boy. He turned the body over. The kid—Rick—stared lifelessly at him.

The gargoyle turned. Neve's eyes were glassy, moist with unshed tears. Father O'Leary's face was pale. The gargoyle looked down at the kid's body again. There was no indication of life; the only sounds from his body were those of dripping blood.

Uglier than burning, he said to himself, examining his bloodied, stone fists.

"Is he dead?" Neve asked, stepping tentatively, nervously closer. The gargoyle nodded. "That's him." She turned away quickly, disgusted. "That was Rick."

"If this is justice," the gargoyle whispered, "then justice has been served."

***

Father O'Leary stared at the kid's body. A moment ago, it had been the body of a demon.

He trembled with the thoughts which flew through his head. Demons, here on earth. Gargoyles to fight them. Nothing protecting mortals. He feared for a world where God allowed demons to roam freely.

What did they do now? Shattered pews surrounded the broken body of a dead boy. Father O'Leary wasn't worried about the potential trouble with his superiors or with the police. He wanted to know how to proceed with covering up this secret while still maintaining the ideals with which he'd lived all his life.

It wasn't something he could do. Father O'Leary's life had been a model of honor and trust, dedication and surrender to God. Now, he saw that God was not to be trusted. How could he trust a being who directed the souls of His own priests into stone statues? No matter how extreme the gargoyle's sin, what justified centuries of this continued existence? What must the gargoyle do to end this torture?

Its demon lay vanquished. Was it wrong to kill a demon? Father O'Leary's head pounded; he closed his eyes to ease the throb. If it wasn't wrong to kill a demon, where did it say this? If it was wrong, why allow demons to exist and create creatures to fight them? This was no predator versus prey, as animals in nature. This was one vicious killer versus another, two men who had destroyed countless lives.

Even in victory, the gargoyle's punishment continued. This was justice? This was the decree of the God Father O'Leary believed in?

Neve Spirito: an innocent girl whom the demon had picked, possibly randomly. Why choose her as victim? Why did such a choice have to be made?

Just a day or two before, Father O'Leary would have said God was great, just, and kind. Tonight, he believed none of these things. God was ruthless, without mercy, and as vicious as either killer in tonight's conflict.

❦

Neve trembled in the front pew. The priest knelt at the altar, praying with his back to the gargoyle. Neve could do nothing but watch the stone man.

He lifted the demon's human body and threw it over his shoulder. Too nonchalantly. Once a murderer, always a murderer? Or did it just get easier as the numbers grew?

In a way, the demon's death, as well as the girl's, rested on Neve's shoulders. She'd named him. With full knowledge of the gargoyle's intention, she had pointed the way.

Yes, the demon would have killed another girl; Neve had left that girl at the hospital, staying long enough to make sure she was okay. Nervous, maybe. Sickened by whatever experiences she had survived. Pale, thin and frightened, but alive and relatively healthy.

Neve considered checking on the girl, but preferred to put this whole thing behind her. Still, she didn't know the ghost wouldn't return with her accusation: "There is no justice." The words still echoed in her mind. The ghost's voice was tiny, showing no sign of anger. It scared the hell out of Neve.

The gargoyle turned to her. "I'll come back."

Neve nodded. She didn't care where the gargoyle planned to dump the body. After he left St. Lazarus', she turned and watched Father O'Leary. She felt numb, not sure of what to do.

The priest knelt with his head bowed, hands folded in prayer. He recited the Our Father continually. He begged for understanding. The facts of the gargoyle and the demon should have confirmed his faith. Like Neve, he trembled.

"You did nothing wrong," Neve told him.

The priest sighed. "We witnessed a miracle. A soldier of Christ and a warrior of Satan, here, within these walls. We witnessed nothing less. Is this a secret, then, that I should carry?" He paused and looked up to the spot the gargoyle had occupied. "I don't think I can stay in this church with him watching over me. I don't know that I could appreciate his form of protection.

"Through God's good graces, you and I both live. But what keeps the gargoyle alive? Is he a gift to us from God, though he himself is cursed with this non-existence? If God is just, if God is kind, why does He leave the man within the gargoyle's body? Why does He allow demons to roam the earth, preying on innocent women like you?" He shook his head. Tears welled in his eyes. "What we witnessed was a miracle of darkness. I can't reconcile what I've seen tonight with my faith. If the gargoyle is forced to exist, if demons walk our streets without constraint, the only conclusions I can reach is God either doesn't exist or He doesn't care."

He shut his eyes and turned back to the altar. Neve approached as he continued. "I believed you when you said you saw a demon, but I believed it existed in your mind. I was wrong in that belief. And, I fear, I may be wrong in others."

She put an arm around the priest, to console the man whose job it was to console. "I think if you sleep, before reaching to any conclusions, you might think more clearly."

Father O'Leary smiled, but shook his head. "My child, I have never seen more clearly."

⚬———⚬

The gargoyle flew low over the water. Far from the city, he dropped the demon's body.

Here, there were no witnesses. Boats sailed in the

distance, and airplanes flew across the sky, but none were close.

He circled the body twice; it floated, disappearing only briefly under the waves. The ocean water was black; never, during life, had the gargoyle seen the ocean. He didn't know its true color. He flew close to it, wishing he could feel its spray on his body. But he felt nothing. He couldn't smell the salt in the air.

He hovered between the ocean and the sky, and turned his gaze on heaven. "Damn you!" he screamed. He rushed upwards. He wanted to fly into heaven and kill God. The gargoyle knew what he'd done. He'd confessed and asked forgiveness. The demon was dead; the gargoyle had fulfilled his role. What more did God want before allowing him into heaven? What more did God demand before releasing him from his sins?

Repent, and you shall be saved! Or, more accurately, repent and you shall still spend eternity in your own private hell! No sense of touch, no sense of smell, unable to walk the streets among men, the gargoyle had no chance for a life; only two people even knew what he was.

Neve Spirito had led him to the demon, but not to salvation. She may not have salvation of her own; he suspected, too late, that she might feel guilt over the demon's death—if only because it had become human after its heart stopped. Had it just been a green-skinned behemoth, not a boy with a face and a human heart under his chest, Neve would not have cared.

And what of Father O'Leary? They might speak

together for hours, days, even years, but for how long would the priest be able to harbor this secret without losing his mind? Five years? Ten? Then: "I've seen God's stone angel come and crush a demon off our streets!" People's faith in him would be lost, and eventually Father O'Leary would leave—unless he lost faith in himself first.

Even if none of these things happened, these people—like everyone else before, and everyone to come—would die. Death existed for everyone—except maybe the gargoyle. Perhaps the gargoyle would survive after mankind crumbled to dust. What then? Would the other gargoyles, and the other creatures who walked only at night to hide their differences in the darkness, finally be freed of their immemorial prisons?

For one hundred years, he had sat in that church, every day a burden. Alone with his thoughts, alone with his memories and imagination, he'd been imprisoned with his guilt. Because there were no other gargoyles. There were probably no other demons, either; the world had moved away from the supernatural. It had moved away from God, or God from it. Perhaps God had forgotten him; the punishment had been meant to end, but God no longer looked in upon the earth. God no longer watched, no longer acted. Maybe another planet, floating around one of those billions of stars, held God's newest creations, whereas the earth was inhabited only by His failures.

Maybe God was dead.

The gargoyle raced to the sky. With all his speed

and every ounce of strength, he flung his stone body high above the water. The atmosphere thinned. He saw millions more stars than he'd ever seen from the ground, even in his sleeping, ghost-like form. But he felt no different. The air, or lack thereof, had no effect on him.

High enough, the gargoyle would confront God Himself. How dare He send the diseases, the weapons of destruction, and on top of that *demons* to plague humanity? That was no God of mercy!

There were so many things the gargoyle wanted to do. He wanted to love again. He wanted to breathe the summer air. He wanted to taste strawberries and a woman's kiss. He wanted to be loved, not feared. The body God had given him was grotesque, a beautiful example of horror at its most potent, and allowed none of this. Even the demon, whose very existence created terror, had feared the gargoyle.

The gargoyle climbed higher over the earth. There was little air here. There were a thousand shooting stars, tiny slivers of light cutting the sky. Some were near him. They fell toward and around him, as if saying, "Go back, this is not your path. The universe is against you." There was a sound, a streaking hiss unlike anything he'd ever heard. But there were no angels, no gates leading to heaven, no saints beckoning him. There was only darkness. Here, loneliness weighed even more heavily upon him; there were no people, no noises of any earth he ever knew, just the strange sounds of dust falling from space.

The gargoyle screamed again. No words this time, just all his anger and frustration and regret embodied in one unheard sound.

When it was done, he glided slowly back to earth: a lonely, solitary earth, hanging in the midst of something much vaster than he'd ever imagined. Earth floated alone in this corner of its universe, just as the gargoyle stood alone in his church.

CHAPTER TWELVE

Gus wandered into another familiar alley. He hadn't seen anything new tonight. There was nothing in the world he didn't recognize. He had seen everything through God's eyes. The red blanket over his vision was the price of seeing into the divine.

Angels walked the earth. He had seen three: one in stone, one with clouds as hair, and a third which had intervened to protect him from the kid. They'd gifted him with God's eyes. He looked at a girl on the streets and saw the woman who would be inaugurated as President in 2044. He glanced at a young man and saw him laying on his deathbed, grandchildren at his side. He saw, in a taxi driver, the man who would save a young girl's life by running into a burning building three weeks from today. The driver would inhale too much smoke and die three days later in a hospital. Gus looked at a police officer and saw him pulling his gun on another officer to prevent the other from beating a confession from an innocent man.

Gus enjoyed his new vision, but didn't know what to do with it. There was a divine purpose which he hadn't yet recognized. When God was ready, He would send another angel to show Gus the path.

They no longer concerned Gus. He recognized *them* on sight, more easily than before, and no longer worried about whether a person worked for *them*.

He bumped something with his feet. The kid lay at

his feet; Gus had wandered back to the alley in which he'd been reborn.

Jesus had been reborn. He rose from the dead after three days. Had three days past since Gus was beaten to death? He knew he hadn't died; the angel rescued him on the edge of death. If the kid had hit him once more, Gus might have died. Then, Gus would be talking with God rather than seeing with *His* eyes.

Gus looked up. A black iron fire escape climbed the apartment building. A man sat there. His legs hung over the edge, between railings, and he grinned at Gus.

With God's eyes, Gus saw that the man wore false flesh. He was something other than human. He was the angel who had stopped the kid from killing him.

"I owe you thanks," Gus said.

The man shook his head. "You owe me nothing," he said. "I only did what I do. Just as I shall continue."

"God granted me a gift."

"God grants no gifts," the man told him. "Whatever you have, you've earned. Whatever you have, you fought for. Nothing was given. There is no God to give you gifts."

"Of course there's a God," Gus told him. "He's given me His eyes."

"What do you see, then, when you look at me?" the man asked. "Do you see my son?"

"You have no son," Gus said, but that wasn't quite right. "You had a son. No more." Gus looked down at his feet, and then up at the man again. "What happened?"

"He asked for my help," the man said. "I failed him."

"You helped me."

"I expected you to die," the man said. "Not much of a challenge." He closed his eyes. Gus stared, hardly able to understand. When the man opened his eyes again, they glowed red. "You see," he told Gus, "there may be no angels. But there are demons."

Gus stepped back. "You're testing me."

The man laughed. His skin bubbled, cracked. All of his skin: arms, legs, face. There was no smoke, no sound. A sickly gel oozed from the cracks. In less than a minute, the man changed into the green-skinned angel. Demon? His eyes were red. He had doubled in size. His legs expanded so greatly, the railings of the fire escape twisted and snapped. Wings expanded behind him, making him even larger. He jumped from the fire escape, shattering what was left of it, and landed within arm's length of Gus.

"You saved me, granted me God's eyes, just to kill me?" Gus asked.

"I'd apologize," the man-demon said, "but I'm really not sorry."

Gus tilted his head, exposing his neck, and allowed the demon's talon to slice through his throat. There was no pain, just a quick flash of hot followed by wet. A lot of wet. He smiled.

"The world is still red," Gus said. He dropped to his knees; he had no strength, and the world turned quickly from red to black. An image flashed through his head: a sword and a cross and a statue of the Virgin Mary. He saw broken glass, all the angels which had visited Gus, and a priest. "I see your blood," Gus whispered.

Concrete cooled his cheek. Strange, he thought there'd be pain as death took him. He wondered, too, why he saw no light yet? Where was God and heaven? Where were the angels to lead him into everlasting life? Ah, there.

The sun had already risen when the gargoyle returned to the church. Father O'Leary sat alone in the front pews. The demon's blood had been cleaned and the damaged pews removed.

The priest turned slowly, saw the gargoyle and sighed. "She's gone home."

"To sleep, I hope," the gargoyle said. "The haunting should be over now."

"Perhaps," the priest said. He turned back to the altar and said nothing more.

The gargoyle watched for a moment. Something had changed. It was more than the priest's quickened heart rate or his fast breathing. There was something missing, something which had always been there. Something the gargoyle couldn't quite understand.

One thing he understood, though, was the need for secrecy. To be seen was to be persecuted. Already, perhaps, too many people knew he existed. He couldn't lower that number. He refused to hurt anyone else.

Especially not Neve Spirito, blood of his blood, child of his children with Magdelina. Five centuries separated Magdelina and Neve, but they were still so much the same. He could never repeat that error, killing the woman he loved. He could never repeat that sin. He had paid quite enough already.

The gargoyle settled into his position above the door. Below, the demon's bag of weapons, even the chipped stone, had been removed. Perched, hidden again from the eyes of modern Inquisitors, the gargoyle focused his attention on the praying priest.

Father O'Leary's hands were folded just the same; actually, they were not folded, but placed palm to palm against each other, so his fingers stretched toward heaven. He trembled. He prayed, quietly mouthing the word's of the Lord's Prayer. Still?

The Bible was shut, laying next to him. The gargoyle saw only part of it at the end of the pew. There, on top of the Bible, the gargoyle saw what was missing from Father O'Leary: his white, priestly collar rested on the book.

The gargoyle wanted to say something, but already there were two parishioners at the door. They laughed loudly, talking about one of the women's children as they pushed through the door.

Father O'Leary, too, heard them. Rather than face his congregation, he scooped up his Bible and collar and disappeared through the side door. Only the candles were lit. The first rays of dawn hadn't quite reached the stained glass window so the women missed their priest's escape.

Should he do something? He knew no way to comfort Father O'Leary; only God could do that now, and He had already failed one of them tonight.

Instead, the gargoyle closed his eyes to sleep, hoping to visit his Neve. She was not Magdelina; she was not, and couldn't be, his lover. Yet she was Magdelina in so many ways. Was it her eyes, a blue unmatched even by the clearest of skies, which held him? They were the same eyes which, over five hundred years ago, had led him to break his vows. There was a time when he'd had beliefs, morals, a conscience. Now, instead, there was regret, frustration, and anger. There was fear, too, that he might live forever. He might fall in love yet again, and watch his loved ones grow old and die as his stone face never aged. He feared that he might care about someone who would, like Neve one day, die.

⌗

Sleeping, the gargoyle floated through the streets. He didn't know if his mind or his spirit moved, or if it was just his imagination. He had a physical effect; Neve had felt his touch once before. He was invisible, in whatever form this was, and physically little more than a cold sensation.

Perhaps this existence was better than his stone body. Maybe, to achieve heaven, he needed to let go of this world completely, go against every instinct which screamed not to stray too far from his earthly body or leave it unguarded for too long. *Unguarded against what?* Again, a question he couldn't answer.

He visited the ocean first. He avoided the place he'd dropped the demon; he wanted to see the ocean's color, feel its strength. He accomplished only half this. In a small way, it satisfied him to see the brilliant dark blues of the sea.

He returned to land and went quickly to Neve Spirito's apartment. He thought to watch over and protect her. His blood ran through her veins; he owed at least this much to himself, and to Magdelina. What had Neve done since leaving the church, he wondered? Did she sleep? Did the ghost still speak to her?

In this ethereal form, the gargoyle moved through the walls as though they didn't exist. He passed into Neve's apartment through the window. He followed the sound of water to another room.

Here, Neve scrubbed under the stream of a shower. Her silhouette painted the curtain.

The steam was thick in this room; it hung in the air and clung to the mirror and window. The gargoyle moved closer to Neve, curious to see if her body was as identical to Magdelina's as it appeared. The shapes were all the same: the curves of hips and breasts; the long, slender arms and legs. Even the way Neve moved her hands across her body, cleaning herself, reminded the gargoyle of Magdelina's hands moving across her own body. And his.

He passed through the curtain, under the steamy water and behind Neve. He stared, for only a moment, and found one physical difference between Neve and Magdelina. At the small of her back, Neve's flesh was soft, smooth, unblemished. There, Magdelina's body had been marked—but by no means scarred—with a tiny red diamond.

The gargoyle withdrew from the shower, needing to see no more. He wanted to remember Magdelina, not Neve, as the woman he loved. Already, Neve influenced his memories of Magdelina. Perhaps they shared only a few characteristics, and the gargoyle's loneliness accentuated these. Eventually, their faces and bodies would merge; in a hundred years when both women were dead, the gargoyle would have difficulty differentiating between them. This, more than anything else, was the hell to which God had sentenced him.

The water stopped. Neve slid the curtain aside and took a white towel which hung on the wall. She began to dry her hair, softly patting it, and looked directly at the gargoyle. "I can almost see you," she whispered.

The gargoyle smiled; in this form, he felt fingers and toes—not the talons of stone—as though his soul, or whatever part of him it was which traveled, maintained its human form. He preferred that she see him like this, instead of as the statue. "You are too much like Magdelina," he said. Neve stepped out of the shower, sliding the towel over her stomach. She looked again at him, but apparently heard nothing.

"I wish I could speak to you," he said. "I wish I could hold your hand. I wish I were warm, and flesh, rather than the cold, hard stone that I am. If I could give you anything in the world, anything at all, I would give you myself." He left the room, left the apartment, and raced back to the church.

Again in his stone body, he opened his eyes with a start. There were only a few people in the church; Father O'Leary was not among them. *I would give you myself,* he completed the thought, *but who would want me as I am now?*

⸻

Early in the morning, Angie wandered back to the deli. Her mind drifted to Willie again and again, settling sometimes on his face and sometimes on his sandwich and sometimes on his meat. She'd never missed him between visits before. She'd always known he'd be coming back.

A meager three room tenement served as Angie's home. Pictures in her living room displayed a lot of things she'd lost in her life: her first son, dead in Vietnam, in an old brown frame; her husband, gone off to North Carolina with some vixen named Lyn ten or more years ago. A box still carried his love notes.

They'd been beautiful together, a long time ago, just as she and Willie shared beautiful moments today.

Yesterday, she corrected herself. No longer.

She had no pictures, no cards, to remind her.

She cut through an alley, the quickest escape from the apartment she shared only with roaches and memories. Vaguely, she missed the rats: her husband and Willie had been terrible men, but she loved and missed them both.

She slipped, almost smashing her head against the ground. Skulls and concrete didn't mix, though for a moment she thought she might be better off.

Standing, Angie looked at her feet. Catsup? Blood? She slid her shoe against the ground to wipe it off, and saw the trail which led beneath the fire escape.

Suddenly, she knew why Penelope had been without her friend the other night. Gus' eyes bulged, a smile frozen on his face, and his blood already began to dry.

She didn't want to have to be the one to tell Penelope, but someone had to. Calmly, Angie completed her trek to the deli. She called the police from there.

* * *

Neve dressed slowly. Leisurely. Outside, the sun shined. Inside, she looked forward to sleep. She planned to lay on her pillow, shut her eyes, and dream good dreams. No longer would demons interrupt her sleep. The ghost had not appeared since the demon's death. Neve suspected it would never return. Life could return to something closer to normal.

A blank canvas in her living room waited for the image of her gargoyle. In the evening, after she woke, she'd begin. Night was, once before, the time for her creations; she saw no reason for that to change, except that it limited her. She thought, now, she'd quit her job and devote herself full-time to her art. She didn't know what she might paint after the gargoyle: perhaps the girl, the one she had left at the hospital. Except, of course, the girl would appear as she had before Rick took her, vibrant and full of life. Perhaps even the ghost, shimmering with her message, except of course the words would remain only in Neve's memories.

So many images floated through her mind. She might even paint the gargoyle and the demon fighting; despite what she'd initially thought when she saw Rick's broken body on the floor of the church, no guilt belonged to her. Rick had been a monster, regardless of his demonic skin. The ghost hadn't returned since Rick's death. Justice had, in fact, been served.

She'd seen the gargoyle's silhouette in the steam from her shower and strangely felt no sense of violation. Instead, it comforted her to know he watched over her. It was rare that someone got the opportunity to meet an ancestor more than two or three generations removed.

Neve loved the feel of satin against her skin, and more than that, loved the fact that tonight, she could enjoy it as she climbed into bed. Everything about her world had changed, but it was too soon to think about that. Now was time to rest, to recover. When she awoke, with all these events in her past, she would be alone again. Blissfully alone. No visitors in the night, no demons stalking her. No one, but maybe her guardian angel in stone.

She fell asleep immediately when she shut her eyes. A dream came, but it was not what she expected.

It felt too real, being back on the bench in Central Park. She sat up, fearful that maybe she had just woken from a dream, that the gargoyle had never fought the demon and she'd never returned to St. Lazarus'. The sun was high above her. An odd silence pervaded her. To the west, the sun sank quickly behind the tallest of buildings. Shadows stretched, grew, and then all of New York was under a shroud. Neve no longer stood alone.

She turned slowly, quietly, and stared at the demon.

Images from the church returned to her; gargoyle and demon throwing punches until the beast fell, bled, and failed to breathe.

But this was a different creature. He stood taller, broader. His skin was a deep, emerald green, not the sickly color of the dead demon. Its eyes were a bright, luminous red. Solid muscle, it had wings which were wide and powerful. Nothing resembled the little demon which the gargoyle had killed.

He leaned closer. She remembered the voice, so much deeper and more resonant than any words she'd ever heard from Rick. The demon which stalked her, and the demon which was Rick, were not the same. Panic caught her breath.

"Good morning, my beautiful lady," he said, reaching for her hand. She jerked away, but the demon caught her. Its touch felt no different than that of a strong man: hard, tight, warm, not at all slimy as she expected.

"Why do you want me?" she asked.

The demon laughed. "Eventually, I want everyone."

"God is coming!" a voice cried. It was the transient, the other who had called Neve an angel. He stepped closer, threatening the demon. "You can't stand in The Light!"

Startled, Neve woke sitting up in bed. Sweat moistened her satin PJs. Her heart raced, and at first she didn't see that she wasn't alone.

It was not the gargoyle who sat on one of her kitchen chairs next to her bed; she had never seen this man, though he looked vaguely familiar. He smiled. It would have been a lovely smile, except the man had broken into her home and watched her sleep.

"Good morning, my beautiful lady," he said. She knew not just the words, but the voice.

Neve stared at the man, whose face hid the countenance of a demon. He was the creature she'd seen in the alleys. He was the creature who violated her dreams.

"Why me?" she asked. She hid her fear, strengthened by the gargoyle's earlier visit.

He smiled and leaned back. He tilted back an inch or two. "You ask questions to which there are no answers."

She threw her legs off the side of the bed and tried to stand. He moved, swiftly, and placed a hand on her chest. Just under her throat, above her breasts, his fingers sent pulses of revulsion throughout her body. He pushed, without effort, and she fell back onto the bed before she could straighten her knees. "Tonight," he said calmly, "we shall leave here. Until then, we shall spend the remainder of the day together, you and I." He glanced, casually, at the clock on the table. "Not too much longer. You've slept quite a long time. I imagine you've been tired."

She stared at him; even as a human, he spoke with the demon's voice. His eyes were brown, deep and dangerous, revealing everything there was to know about him. She wanted none of it. Though muscular, he was no larger than most men. She might have passed him on the street a thousand times without a second look. But he looked vaguely familiar; it was more than the fact that he was the demon, because he bore no resemblance to the creature of her dreams. "You're Rick's father," she said. The realization deepened her fright.

He nodded. "In the past, yes, I was Rick's father. But you and your friend have changed that, now, haven't you? No longer do I have a son. No, it would seem my family's legacy ends with me.

"You ask me why, but I can't answer that. How did my son choose?" He shook his head. "I don't know even how I choose. I don't question why, and so I have no answer for you. Instead, I give you a question.

"Why do you still breathe? Why did he allow you to live?" He leaned closer, and it felt like the demon leaning closer—because, in fact, it was. "So, perhaps you can provide an answer for me. What reason did my son have to leave you alive?"

Unable to move off the bed, Neve slid closer to the wall—anything to put some distance, no matter how small, between her and the intruder.

"Do you have an answer?"

She looked at the clock and then glanced to the window. She'd slept through the day; outside, the shadows grew long, and the pale moon already hid behind a thin layer of clouds. Full night was less than an hour away.

She nodded. "I think I do."

"Well," the man said, leaning back again, "I think this is something I need to hear."

She looked at him, directly at and through him. "He wanted to die." She narrowed her eyes slightly. "I gave him what he asked for."

The man swung his arm back, shattered the front of her bureau, and jumped to his feet. "Bitch," he spat.

"Just the truth," she said.

"I make you this promise, then," he told her. "You shall join my son, in heaven or hell if you believe in those, though in truth, you shall join him only in death. There is no heaven, woman, and this is hell. Your personal hell ends tonight."

Neve grinned. "'Stop me from sinning,' he told me. 'You are my avenging angel, my only hope.'"

His fists curled at Neve's words. Every muscle in his body tightened, and he exhaled angrily as Neve continued. "'Save her, and save me.' He hated what you gave him. Hated what he was." She embellished, and liked the effect. "He begged to die, begged to be released from what you cursed him with. You, your legacy: he hated it all. I didn't know, then, why he wanted so badly to die. I know now. He hated you, hated becoming you, and knew he could do nothing to prevent it but die."

The man stopped pacing. "I might just kill you here and now."

"And yet you won't," Neve told him, though she really had no way of knowing. "I've given you your answer. Give me mine. You said we would leave here. Where do we go? Why haven't you already killed me?"

She noticed, for the first time—perhaps because he had appeared so invulnerable and no longer clung so strongly to that illusion—tiny streaks of gray in the man's brown hair.

He turned away and looked out the window. "The demon exists only at night. When the sun falls, you and I shall visit God."

The intruder sat back in the chair and watched the light fade through the bedroom window. Neve sat as deep in the furthest corner of the bed as she could reach.

He sat between her and the cracked bureau. A large mirror hung on the wall behind it. In front of that sat a jewelry box. On top of the box, untouched and unnoticed by the man, was the platinum cross Selinda had given Neve: her weapon. Not much of a weapon, but fists alone wouldn't be enough.

She tried not to stare at it. She didn't want the man to notice it. He sat closer to it than she did, watching her through the corner of his eye. A thought passed frequently through Neve's mind, to kick the chair out from under him. It rested on two legs the way he tilted. As simple as that action seemed to be, she saw no benefit in making the attempt. If she knocked him down, if he wasn't quick enough or sensitive enough to predict her move and prevent her, she doubted she'd have time to climb over or around him to reach the cross. More, she doubted the cross posed a great threat to the man; as much damage as she might do with it, he would easily rip it from her hands, and her heart from her chest, before she harmed him enough.

Outside, the sun was nearly gone. Soon, they would visit God, which Neve assumed meant a return to St. Lazarus' and the gargoyle. Vengeance was too simple a motive to dismiss.

"May I dress?" she asked.

A startled expression glazed his eyes. "What?"

"May I dress?" Neve repeated. "Let me have some dignity when we visit God."

"Of course," the man said, motioning to the closet. She rose, walked to her closet—further from the cross, but still a step in the right direction. She slid the door open, quickly found pants and a white blouse. She didn't turn around.

"Some privacy?" she asked.

The man laughed. "Funny," he said.

"I can be humble before God," she said, turning toward him, "but not before you? I can't change my clothes in front of you any more than I could change inside a bar Saturday night."

He looked at her. She felt his eyes run up her legs, stomach and chest. He smiled, and it was the most frightening thing Neve Spirito had ever seen. That smile barely contained anger, amusement, and even vanity. His teeth were jagged, pointed, and locked together as a zipper. His irises were red rubies ablaze.

"It's a shame you must die," he said, standing, "as I find something about you alluring." He stood taller now, broader; his body changed gradually as the sun fell. A full minute passed. The color in his eyes deepened, coated with a rainbow of blood. He turned and walked out of the bedroom.

He didn't shut the door, though, and stood just beyond the doorway with his back to her.

Neve examined his back, saw how easy it would be to plunge the sharp end of the cross between his shoulder blades. If it cut through all his muscle, the dagger might tear his heart.

She pushed the thought away. Locking her eyes on the man's back, she walked slowly to her bureau as she climbed out of her satin pajama bottoms. One foot forward as she stepped into pants. She put the other foot forward. She put her arm through the sleeve of her blouse and picked up the cross.

It warmed her hand and felt hot against her chest when she hung it around her neck. It knew. The cross pulsed against her skin and caught the last sunlight that struggled to reach through her window.

She buttoned her blouse over it and said, "I just need shoes now."

The man turned to look at her. He nodded. "You are quite lovely in white. Like an angel."

She avoided looking at him. Outside, the sun was gone. Its last vestiges of light scattered across the skyline. Neve returned to her closet, unable really to think about what she chose. Behind her, the man's eyes weighed heavily upon her. She felt vulnerable, especially with her back to the demon's father. She grabbed the most comfortable shoes without searching and slipped quickly into them. "I'm ready," she announced, turning.

The demon, no longer man at all, stood outside her bedroom door. "So am I."

<hr />

The sun fell, the church emptied, but the gargoyle didn't rise from his perch. Throughout the day, Father O'Leary had not once come into St. Lazarus'. A deacon had delivered morning mass.

Darkness cloaked the church before it completely covered the city, filtered through the stained glass window above the statues of Jesus and the Virgin Mary. It comforted the gargoyle. For so many years, he had watched without moving, without caring. But now that he had moved, he wanted no part of either life.

It was far too dangerous to exist in this world. There were people—not unlike the person he had once been—who would never rest until they destroyed him. He was too different and too much a sign that God existed. There was no better explanation for a living statue. And before this miracle—curse, perhaps, but who other than the gargoyle himself would see it that way?—could be witnessed by the multitudes, the fearful would destroy what they failed to understand.

It frightened the gargoyle that even one person might see him as a miracle. Already, he had been proclaimed a "stone angel." He preferred anonymity. To this end, he kept his name secret. He was no longer the man whose name he once used; it belonged to someone dead.

If defeating the demon hadn't freed him, the gargoyle feared nothing would. He considered returning to his homeland in Spain, to see if his church, where he'd ended his life, still stood. He wanted to find Magdelina's unmarked grave.

He wouldn't leave without visiting Neve Spirito, face to face, without the pretense of a demon to destroy. He wanted to tell her everything there was to tell. Not Father O'Leary. Not God. There were things he'd failed to admit, even to himself. Why would he tell Neve? The answer was simple enough: he loved her.

That, too, was a reason to leave. It was a love which could neither be returned nor consummated. For more than a hundred years, the gargoyle had sat in this wall without once thinking about the pleasures of the flesh he no longer experienced. Even this was a lie, as he'd thought often of Magdelina and everything they'd shared. But there had never been another woman who intrigued the gargoyle the way Neve did. No one had ever threatened to overshadow the memories of Magdelina which he clung to so tightly.

It was worse, because the gargoyle could share no new experiences with Neve Spirito. He'd only be able to reveal his past sins. He could have nothing new, never again, not while his body prevented him from walking freely in the streets. Solitude didn't exist in this world.

Tonight, he planned to leave. He'd explore the world. If there was no place on land which offered what he needed, he would fly over the oceans until his body failed to support him in the air. Or he'd fly into the sky, up until he melted in the sun.

CHAPTER THIRTEEN

Father O'Leary walked slowly, reluctantly, into St. Lazarus', head tilted down at his feet to avoid the gargoyle. Except for his missing collar, he still wore last night's clothes. Red lines mapped the whites of his eyes. He clutched a Bible so tightly in one hand, his knuckles were as white as Neve Spirito's hair.

The gargoyle came down to greet him. "I don't know what happened," the priest said. His voice was little more than a hoarse whisper. "Two days ago, I believed God was great. I believed He was good." He paused sighed. "You've helped me realize the lie."

"No lie," the gargoyle said.

"No?" the priest asked. "The God I grew up believing in would never force a man to live as you do. The God I believed in was merciful, kind, and forgiving."

"Maybe," the gargoyle suggested, "I must ask to be forgiven."

"You have asked."

The gargoyle shook his head. "We never completed my confession."

Dark circles hung under Father O'Leary's eyes. His hair was uncombed, his face unshaven.

The priest turned away.

"I don't blame you," the gargoyle said. "But I have no one else to tell, no one I can trust with this burden.

"God allows demons to crawl the earth, searching for and destroying the innocent. That woman, Neve Spirito, what did she do to deserve her fate? What sin did she commit, that the demon intruded upon her life?" Words spilled from him quickly, the result of a day's solitary thoughts. "How many more are there, gargoyle? How many other creatures has God sent down to earth? What have we, as a race, done to deserve such harsh punishment?"

The gargoyle smiled sadly. "I know what I, personally, have done. There are, and have been, many others besides me who have acted no less mercilessly."

"She, however, did no such thing."

The priest settled on the pew. His body slumped in exhaustion, but he didn't close his eyes. He refused the luxury of sleep. The Bible rested in his lap. Pages had been torn out and huge sections were missing completely.

"No story in here explains you," Father O'Leary said. "No where does it explain the demon. I've always believed souls not permitted into heaven went instead to hell. I never imagined the devil sent his army to gather those souls and bring them to him early."

After a long pause, during which Father O'Leary stared blankly at his Bible, he spoke again. "I still believe in God. Nothing changed that. I just don't think God is what I'd believed Him to be."

A high-pitched explosion erupted in the church. Glass showered them. The gargoyle spread his wings to protect the priest from falling glass and metal. The shards were a rainbow of dark colors. A second sound, glass raining on wood and stone, quickly followed. The stained glass window, once a beautiful rendition of Christ on the cross, cascaded in a thousand tiny pieces.

The gargoyle looked up to see what had shattered the window. It came in with a wind, extinguishing most of the candles and throwing the falling glass into miniature whirlwinds. It came in loud and fast.

By the time the gargoyle saw what it was, it struck him!

The creature—another demon, bigger than the first—threw the gargoyle through an entire row of pews. They shattered as he slid across the floor. A piece of stone, once a part of the gargoyle's face, clattered off at an angle.

The demon stood taller than the gargoyle, broader, and its flesh was a dark, rich green. Its eyes cast a red incandescence over the whole church, they were so bright. In one hand, it carried Neve Spirito. In the other, it bared only its claws: three of them, six inches long, and a shorter spike as thumb.

It lifted Neve Spirito over its head and turned to the priest. "Forgive me, Father," it said with a soft, deep voice. "I am about to sin."

The gargoyle rose to his feet. The demon had thrown him a full fifty yards, too great a distance to cross before the creature tore Neve in half.

The demon dropped her—harshly—on one of the remaining pews at the front of the aisle. It grinned and narrowed its eyes. "Are you ready, gargoyle?"

The gargoyle nodded, and the demon rushed forward. It moved five times faster than the first demon. It ran a few steps, rose slightly in the air, and turned completely over so that it flew parallel to the ground. The demon reached down as it passed over the gargoyle and extended eight talons.

The gargoyle threw his fist forward, hitting the demon between the eyes even as its claws sliced the gargoyle's shoulders. Scraped stone made a sickening screechy sound, and slivers of gray rock fluttered from him.

He turned; the demon flipped, landing directly in front of him, and reached for the gargoyle's face with both hands. A disappointingly small amount of green blood dribbled from the demon's eye.

The gargoyle stepped back to avoid the assault, then moved forward with his own. The demon wrapped its wings around him, drew them together, and squeezed.

Inches separated their faces. The gargoyle's twisted stone facade and the demon's glowing eyes were both designed for intimidation, locked together too closely for either to clearly see the other.

The gargoyle spread his own wings. Stone ripped through the bone and flesh of the demon.

It screamed. The demon expelled the gargoyle and climbed into the air. It flew clumsily, but quickly compensated for its torn wing. Blood rained like the glass only a moment before. The wound, however, was already repairing itself. Ripped pieces grew toward each other. It might take a few minutes, but the gargoyle found its speed and efficiency in repairing itself uncomfortable. The other demon had displayed no signs of regeneration as they fought.

"In the name of the Father," Father O'Leary said, far away and almost unheard. "In the name of the Son, and of the Holy Spirit, this is a house of God, demon! Be gone!"

The demon glanced at him, allowing the gargoyle the same momentary distraction.

Father O'Leary still clutched the Bible. He stood over Neve Spirito, who had not risen from where she'd been dropped. Blood stained the priest's face and arms: cuts from the shower of glass. There was anger, fury, in his eyes.

The gargoyle had no time to fear for Neve Spirito. Her breaths came raggedly, but her heart pounded fiercely—not the heart of someone about to die.

The gargoyle shot into the air and slashed the demon's belly. His claws left three red lines on the demon, who spun and kicked with both legs.

The gargoyle dropped a few yards through the air.

⚬―――⚬

Pain greeted Neve before she opened her eyes. Tiny, sharp pains extended throughout her back, down her legs, under her arms, and even under her head. They were external, something pressed against her. Her head and back ached from the fall. She remembered, far too clearly, the demon crashing through the stained glass window and dumping her. Shards of that glass must have been under her, the source of some of the pain.

She opened her eyes and saw the cathedral ceilings. Beneath them, and beneath the jagged opening which was once a window, the gargoyle rushed up at the demon.

They collided. She couldn't close her eyes, though she didn't want to see the gargoyle fight for her. And it was for her that he fought. The demon's son had chosen her as his angel—as the gargoyle, later, had also done—and she'd failed them. The ghost, and the second demon, existed because Neve had failed. If she'd just pulled the trigger, tightened her finger enough to send a single bullet into Rick's skull, the gargoyle would not be locked in a death dance with another demon.

That the bullet might not have killed him, or that the weapon wasn't even loaded beyond his first shot, weren't considerations. He'd asked for death, and nothing less would have satisfied him. Nothing.

He'd found his death. Now, the father came to avenge it. The father had burst into the church with one intention: destroying the gargoyle that took his son's life. Neve and the priest were secondary. Incidental. Almost worthless. But they, too, would die.

Closer than the fight, the priest stood over her. He held a Bible. Sweat rolled off his forehead as he stared at the battle with clenched jaw and fist.

She hoped the gargoyle could win. Prayer, however, was not an option. If God allowed this demon into His house, permitted this desecration of a supposedly sacred sanctuary, why would He interfere to save her now? Why would He interfere to save the gargoyle, who had once sentenced heretics to death in His name, when He had already allowed the gargoyle to suffer for a hundred years?

Neve touched her chest. More precisely, she touched the platinum cross which hung between her breasts. It was her weapon. It might become her salvation. It was hot on her skin now, not just warm. It burned its shape into her flesh. There was something special about this weapon. Even if the gargoyle's stone claws only scratched the demon, this weapon would do much more. She regretted not having used it before, despite how narrow a chance she'd been given.

* * *

The demon pursued the gargoyle downward. It swung both fists, kicked both feet, pushed lower and lower until the gargoyle crashed into the floor.

It swung with open hands and scraped its claws across the gargoyle's face and body. Though he felt no pain, the gargoyle saw flakes of stone being stripped away. He imagined what it must feel like to have his skin peeled. The demon's attacks were so swift, he had no time for any other reaction.

The wood beneath the gargoyle cracked, but he didn't feel how much—if at all—it bent. Lack of feeling gave him the advantage of not feeling pain, but it took other things away. He hoped what he gained outweighed what he lost. He pushed upwards with everything he had.

He didn't really know that it was everything, because his muscles didn't strain. He felt no tension, no exertion. He took no breaths, and so was never winded. He just fought, blind of his most important senses.

Without pain, the gargoyle couldn't comprehend the extent of damage done to him. When he heard a piece of stone hit the floor, he had to look at his hands to confirm his fists were intact. Were those pieces of his face which fell from him?

The gargoyle's push upwards sent the demon spinning into the air. Though blood stained its face, body, and wings, the wounds were no longer visible. They closed as quickly as the gargoyle created them.

The demon wasted no time; it lunged with another attack. It threw the gargoyle into the altar.

The altar shattered. The red velvet knee rests at the foot of the altar broke and flew away. The marble statue of Christ shook. The statue of Mary fell, spraying a thousand slivers of marble over the glass which already blanketed the floor.

Father O'Leary, unable to release his Bible, repeated his line over and over like a chant. "In the name of the Father, the Son, and the Holy Spirit, I cast you out, demon! In the name of the Father, the Son, and the Holy Spirit, I cast you out!"

The demon's red eyes glowed as brightly as ever. The other creature's eyes had dimmed as it neared death. If this demon couldn't die, it would eventually break the gargoyle into enough pieces to incapacitate him.

What would life be like, then? With which piece would the gargoyle's soul remain? The largest chunk of the head? The heart? Would he still hear, or see, or would he be trapped with only his thoughts? Was this the fate the demon demanded for him?

The demon flew toward the gargoyle. The gargoyle flew toward the demon, all claws and talons extended. Fury fueled them both.

The gargoyle spun to one side before they crashed. He grabbed the demon's wing and pulled. Bone cracked. Blood sprayed the air; they were near the ceiling, near the shattered remnants of the stained glass window, and blood splashed outside as well as in. The demon tumbled, side to side and head over feet, through the air. The wing, almost as large as the broken window, came completely off its body.

The demon screamed, drowning out all other sounds. Glass in the window frame cracked at the sound. Little remained, but what was left splintered and fell.

The gargoyle tossed the demon's wing through the window. Already, the wound on the demon's body began to heal. This, however, would take much longer than a few scratches across the belly.

The wing itself had shown no sign of healing, so the gargoyle was confident it wouldn't grow into a second demon. One demon—and this was the second—was more than enough.

The demon crashed to the floor. The gargoyle rushed after it. Extensive damage, like the removal of appendages, might destroy the demon. If the wounds were too great and too numerous, there must be a point when healing became impossible.

The gargoyle lunged, his open fist like a sword, and pushed his claws into the demon's chest and out its back.

"You," the demon said, "do not regenerate." It lifted both hands and brought them down solidly on the gargoyle's arm.

The gargoyle pulled back, withdrawing his arm from the demon's chest, but not before a large chunk of stone was severed. It bothered him, feeling no pain; that should have hurt.

Since it didn't, the gargoyle swung the jagged edge of his broken arm into the demon's face. The creature ducked and brought its fists up again at the gargoyle's arm. Another chunk flew free.

They were small pieces, no larger than a man's fist, but a finite number of those pieces made the gargoyle whole. Still, the demon's wounds were great, and the intensity of its crimson eyes wavered, so the gargoyle swung again.

Again. And again.

He heard the priest's words, that continuing prayer, and realized that the battle moved too close to the two very vulnerable, very mortal witnesses. He lifted the demon by its throat and threw it toward the rear of the church—away from Neve and Father O'Leary.

The demon hit the doors; they buckled under its weight, but didn't break. There was enough already broken within the church. The demon looked at the hole in its chest, and then to the gargoyle's eyes.

Already, the hole had begun to close!

The gargoyle threw all his weight and momentum into a flying kick. He caught the side of the demon's head as it tried to duck; the force knocked it off its feet.

The gargoyle landed on the demon, punching and punching, swinging wildly, not caring where he hit so long as it was the demon's flesh.

The demon curled into a ball, protecting its face with its arms. The gargoyle tore at those arms, ripping its green flesh and spilling its emerald blood.

Then, the impossible happened. The demon swung one arm, striking the gargoyle in the chest, and sent him flying across the church. The gargoyle crashed into the statue of Jesus at the altar; it shattered behind him. Pain. Glorious, powerful, *pain* rushed through the gargoyle's chest.

He looked down, and what he saw was even more incredible: blood. His blood, seeping from his chest. Gray blood, a lighter shade than his rock body. It was molten, liquid rock. It moved, slowly, *but it bled*!

The gargoyle touched his chest and felt the warm, sticky blood on the tips of his claws. Felt the blood. He smelled it, as well, and so many other scents: the clean body of Neve Spirito, the unwashed odor of Father O'Leary, the rank stink of the demon's open wounds. The scent of candles, no longer burning, still drifted in the air. Stone dust, wood dust, and wine—the blood of Christ—filled the gargoyle's nose.

He touched his mouth. He felt the rough texture of his blood and tasted its bitter, sour flavor. An instant later, he realized what this meant. He may not know the cause or the purpose, but the gargoyle understood one consequence: when the demon hit him again, he would feel it. And he would hurt.

<hr />

Neve Spirito jumped to her feet. Glass crunched beneath her shoes. Father O'Leary stopped his chant and joined her in staring at the gargoyle. Even the demon stared, motionless. Certainly, it had never expected to draw the gargoyle's blood.

But what else could that be seeping from the hole in the gargoyle's chest? Gray blood. The blood of a rock. Blood, drawn by a demon.

"He bleeds," the priest whispered, dropping his Bible.

"He *bleeds*," the demon repeated, relishing the word as it eagerly escaped its tongue.

The gargoyle looked to Neve, and then to the demon. Was there fear in his face? Pain? Did he feel that? She'd thought he was immune to pain.

Something else caught Neve's eye. Something no one else seemed to notice. Not the demon. Not the priest. Not even the gargoyle, who laid next to it. But there it was, its glitter lost in the sparkling glass all about the floor.

The demon rushed toward the gargoyle. There was no closing her eyes anymore. Neve didn't have the luxury of letting things happen to her now; it was time to make things happen. She stepped closer.

The priest grabbed her shoulder. "No, child,"

Neve shrugged him off and took another step.

The demon swung at the gargoyle, throwing his face backwards again. Pieces of the gargoyle were scattered about the church, yet the gaping holes in the demon's skin continued to close. "Stop!" she yelled.

By some miracle, the demon obeyed. It stood over the gargoyle, who bled now from his chest, mouth, and the side of his head. It held the gargoyle by the throat and had a fist drawn back to punch. Four six-inch claws were extended, chisels the demon used to carve the gargoyle's new, more grotesque features.

"Don't," Father O'Leary said behind her, but she ignored him.

"Stop," she said again to the demon. "You want your revenge, take it on me. I led him to your son. I asked him to save me. You've shown that he can't do that, so leave him. Take me."

"Child," Father O'Leary whispered.

The demon regarded her with a smile. "In time."

The gargoyle kicked with both legs, throwing the demon off him.

"There!" Neve yelled, running closer and pointing to the shattered statue of Mary.

The gargoyle followed Neve Spirito's finger to the pieces which once were Mary; he hoped that she, the statue, had not been occupied by a soul as his inhabited the gargoyle. If she had been, he hoped she'd have done something to stop her fall.

In the midst of the rubble, he saw what Neve pointed at. Six feet long, two inches wide at the base, the sword's hilt was a foot long—as though made for the gargoyle's hand.

The demon saw it, too, but couldn't react before the gargoyle picked it up. He wielded it as a master, needing only one stone hand to hold the gleaming weapon. He ignored the pain—it was new to him, but now was not the time to relish in new sensations. Now was time to rid the world of a demon.

He rushed forward. He tasted blood on his lips and saw it as it dribbled across his eye—he felt it there, too, hot and stinging, but he thrust all that aside. He swung the sword. The demon put up its arm and used its claws to block the weapon.

The blade sliced through the three claws in its path. They flew away, clattered, and sounded much like the fallen chunks of the gargoyle's body. The blade glimmered as it cut. The demon's eyes flickered. For a moment—only a moment—the eyes stared lifelessly.

The demon screamed and raced awkwardly into the air. Its wing had not finished repairing itself. The hole in its chest, too, was unclosed—but closing. It drew its wounded hand to its chest, so the gargoyle couldn't see it.

The sword reflected a light not visible in the church. A gleam moved like ripples across its surface.

It was not the metals the gargoyle had ever seen in a sword before. It was something like silver, with a touch of white. It became an extension of his arm, not because of the gargoyle's skill with a sword—he had none from life as a priest—but because of its skill with the arm that wielded it. The sword guided his hand more than he guided it, as though alive. Which was no more abstract a notion than that of a stone gargoyle which pulled itself free of the wall to fly.

The gargoyle rose into the air. The sword led his charge.

The demon rushed to meet the gargoyle, holding his one hand to his chest; the claws, on the floor of the church, showed no sign that they might grow.

Gargoyle and demon struck in midair. The sword pierced the demon's chest, as the demon's claws pierced the gargoyle. They bounced off each other and plummeted to the floor.

Pain wracked the gargoyle's body. Landing in the center of the littered apse, the gargoyle screamed in agony. The sword tumbled away, lost in an overwhelming rise of pain. He didn't need to look at his chest to feel the hole there. Cracks spread from the hole, stretching up to his neck and down to his legs. The gargoyle didn't need to see the piece of stone which was once his stomach and chest to know it was no longer a part of him.

He couldn't force the pain aside. He tried to raise himself off the floor, but his arms struggled to support him. With his blood, strength flowed out of the gargoyle. The pain threatened to make him black out. Darkness crept into the corners of his eyes. In the center of his vision now was the stained glass window, what remained of it, high above him. It wavered and trembled: a function of the gargoyle's perception, not reality.

He tilted his head and hoped to see the demon hurt more extensively.

It stood near the foot of the altar, its back to Neve Spirito and Father O'Leary but only a few feet from them. The first hole the gargoyle had created in the demon's chest was mostly healed. Even its wing was nearly complete again. But the sword's cut, a long, deep incision between its ribs, bled freely. A piece of the sword had broken off in the demon's chest. The creature grabbed it with both hands—six inches protruded from his flesh—and yanked it free with a scream.

Then, it turned its attention to the gargoyle. It tossed the piece of the sword to the side, where it vanished quickly in the rubble of stone, glass, wood, and marble. Its eyes were a weak red but hadn't faded completely. For one second, earlier, when the gargoyle first cut him with the sword, they had died.

Again, the gargoyle tried to stand, but his arms failed and he fell back to the floor.

The demon's wounded talons hadn't begun to rebuild themselves, and the slash in his chest didn't appear to be closing. But if that was all the damage the gargoyle had done before being defeated, it wasn't enough. The demon staggered, but still walked, while the gargoyle couldn't rise from the ground.

The demon's body faded; it closed in on itself, imploding, and in as much time as it took to open a door, a man's body replaced it. He stepped closer, tilted his head from side to side, and then reversed the transformation.

The demon grew out of the man's body. To quicken the healing process? When it was fully a demon again, the talons were not as short.

The gargoyle tried to rise again. The demon laughed, a choked sound, and stepped closer.

Father O'Leary hated the demon's laughter. If this was how it ended, with the gargoyle paralyzed and the demon replacing its wounded parts, then God couldn't exist. He needed no further proof.

He wanted to die next. It was cowardly, but Father O'Leary didn't want to see the girl die. Watching the gargoyle fall had been hard enough.

For a moment, he had believed God existed. The gargoyle's blood suggested an end to his torment. That end approached quickly. But to end the suffering of the gargoyle, and still allow the demon to exist—this, Father O'Leary couldn't understand. Yes, God worked in mysterious ways. Yes, it was wrong of him to question The Lord's actions. But the God Father O'Leary believed in was supposed to be just.

Father O'Leary was ready to abandon his beliefs. What else was left to do? If the beast let him live, how could he come into St. Lazarus' and pray to a God who had failed him? How could he ignore his new beliefs?

He couldn't. The battle between gargoyle and demon ended with the demon victorious. Humanity suffered the loss. Once, Father O'Leary might have prayed for salvation, but he now doubted God would listen or care.

The demon's laugh sickened Neve. It laughed its deep, echoing laugh, and there was no other sound in the church. The gargoyle tried, and failed, to rise from the floor. During the demon's transformations from beast to man to beast again it had replaced some of its lost flesh.

She stepped closer, hoping her footsteps would go unheard beneath the demon's laughter. It changed to a man again, and then back to a demon. Each transformation brought it closer to being the whole demon that had smashed through the window.

The piece of the sword the demon had pulled from his chest was lost in the church; though it may be found later, there was no time now. It didn't matter. She saw the damage it had done to the beast, saw how the creature almost didn't recover from the attack. The blade was not a normal sword made of normal metal, but something more substantial, something more ethereal: platinum.

She pulled the cross out of her shirt. Behind her, the priest objected but said nothing. She was too close; the demon needed only to turn, or spread its wings, to kill her.

It changed again, taking the form of the man she'd found upon waking from what would be her last nightmare. She leapt—she might get no other chance—and plunged the dagger end of the cross deep into the man's back.

He threw her backwards, into the waiting arms of Father O'Leary. The man spun, changing, and the cross vanished within its demonic flesh. It stepped closer, clenching its fists—with nearly complete talons in the wounded hand—and flexing its wings.

Instead of reaching for her, though, the demon reached for its back and screamed. It clawed at its own flesh, digging for the cross enveloped by its skin in the transformation. It screamed, rose into the air, and screamed again. Spinning, it tore at its back, unable to reach the place she'd sunk the weapon.

The demon fell to the ground, on its knees, and howled so loudly and deeply that Neve's bones vibrated and the remaining glass windows of the church shattered.

Red faded from its eyes, replaced by a normal, human brown. The demon's face folded into that of a man. He stared at her, crawled closer on his knees, and fell on his face.

The cross, coated with blood, glimmered in his back.

Neve ran to the gargoyle. He tried to sit up but didn't have the strength. She knelt, touched the one cheek which was not shattered, and turned to Father O'Leary. "What do we do?"

Father O'Leary stepped over the fallen body of the demon, now lifeless in the center of the church, and knelt next to Neve. "Lord," he said, bowing his head, "please hear me now, even if you never hear me again. Release this man, this sinner who has confessed his sins and begged forgiveness, from his prison. Show mercy on his soul."

Then the priest closed his eyes and cried.

⚯

The gargoyle tried to smile. His broken and cracked face failed in this attempt, but he tried. He looked up at

Neve, whose hand was so soft and warm against his cheek, and at Father O'Leary, whose tears were not quite silent.

He reached up, touching Neve's cheek. His hand was cracked. Pieces were missing, but still he felt Neve's tender skin. This, not the pain, was why God had returned his sense of touch.

The taste of blood was strong. Neve's scent: clean, sweaty with exertion, and now coated with a thin layer of the demon. God had given men noses for this purpose. Why had He given the gargoyle a nose, after a hundred years? Why give the gargoyle pain and touch when a century had passed without such privileges? And it was, indeed, a privilege, to be able to touch once again.

"He's dead?" the gargoyle asked.

Neve nodded, and in her softest, sweetest voice, said, "He is." She smiled down at him and closed her eyes.

The gargoyle laid his head back. "I think," he said, softly, "that I am, too."

The priest smiled down at him. He knew this was what the gargoyle wanted: an end to damnation. An end to existence as the gargoyle.

Tears spilled from Neve's eyes. They were silent, gentle streams of purity in a church where there was nothing pure anymore. Even the statue of Mary, Virgin Mother of God, laid broken on the floor.

"This is good," the gargoyle told her, but he didn't know if she heard. He closed his eyes, and thought back on the things he had done. How many lives had they just saved? How many victims of these two demons would not die because the demons were gone? How many other demons were there that he couldn't defeat?

The fight had left him. He hoped there was at least one life saved for every one of the 467 people he had killed; he added the demons to his original count. "You, daughter of my daughter," he said to Neve, "are my redemption."

"You are mine," Neve answered, closing her eyes. She didn't know if the gargoyle would die, though. Would he be trapped, eternally, in a broken stone body, suffering the pains inflicted upon him by a demon blessed with death? She touched the wound on his chest, the first wound to bleed, and felt the sticky, warm blood. She leaned closer to the gargoyle's face and touched her lips against his cheek. Grotesque and broken as he may be, she kissed him gently. The stone, jagged and rough, didn't hurt her.

The gargoyle removed his hand from Neve's cheek and dropped it slowly next to his body. There was no strength in him anymore.

She followed his gaze up and beyond her, at the circular hole high above the altar. Once a window, it was now nothing more than an opening. The image of Christ appeared there, as though the window had never fallen, illuminated from behind by a bright, white light.

In the light, the gargoyle cracked and broke. Beneath the stone facade there was the body of man: naked, shriveled, bleeding, but a man. He looked at Neve, then Father O'Leary, with a smile true and radiant—a light of its own.

The pieces of the gargoyle dissolved into dust.

The light was gone, as were all remains of the gargoyle's stone body. The man, frail and no longer a statue, laid there. He tilted his head to Father O'Leary and said, "Our God *is* merciful, Father." He smiled, laying his head back, and closed his eyes.

Neve rocked him in his arms, wishing he had time to live as a man rather than a gargoyle. But that time had been five hundred years ago. He'd had his time and used it poorly.

His body faded into just the image, insubstantial, and it floated like smoke through her arms and out of the church. Neve closed her eyes, rocking back and forth. Through tears, she smiled; the gargoyle had obtained his redemption.

A minute, a day, a year later—Neve no longer understood time, as she held the dead flesh of the gargoyle—Father O'Leary began to pray. "Our Father, who art in heaven, hallowed be thy name...."

EPILOGUE

Chloe woke early in the morning and rushed to the bathroom. Sometimes, her stomach hurt too much to get up, but she hadn't gotten sick in bed. Not yet.

This was an early morning ritual now. Every day, for the past month, she rushed to the bathroom immediately upon waking. And later in the morning. And early in the afternoon. A thousand times a day: sometimes just to pee, other times because she was sick, and other times because the pain was just too much.

She didn't see many people anymore. She had no friends. She'd given up her apartment and lived with Daddy now. He suffered from the bane of every father, always wanting to look out for "Daddy's Little Girl."

He couldn't throw her out. They both knew that the morning he picked her up at the hospital.

Rick was gone. He wasn't coming back this time. His apartment was untouched, his car sat abandoned near the hospital. She had gotten into the computer at his warehouse and found files on almost a hundred men and women. She'd found his e-mail and thousands of stored letters. She didn't respond to any; some wanted to meet him, some wondered why he'd never shown up, others were worried that he'd stopped answering. Well, Rick was dead and wouldn't be coming back to bother anyone anymore.

She had his rings in her room at Daddy's house. Each ring meant something. They were connected to the women who had worn them. They represented their lives. Rick had kept information about each of them, but Chloe hadn't found all the stories yet. The files confused her and, as yet, she'd only found one story about a ring, an engagement ring. The girl, whose wedding was planned a month from today, in fact, wouldn't be getting married. The files included a picture of her and also a picture of the woman with the white hair who had taken Chloe to the hospital.

That woman didn't have a name in the computer. It said only "Failed Angel of Mercy." No dates were connected to her; all the other pictures had dates of birth and death.

Chloe hadn't found her own file yet, but she hadn't given up hope. These other woman, after all, were only his toys. She was much more than that. She was the demon's lover.

She would be the mother of the demon's only child.

He grew within her, kicking already and screaming inside her mind. Daddy believed it was a child of rape, and she preferred it that way. He asked her, daily, if she wanted to abort it. She refused. She insisted she'd put it up for adoption, but found no comfort in the idea of killing it.

Daddy didn't know, but it was all Rick had left her. Daddy didn't need to know. He paid her medical bills, bought her clothes and food, and believed she had given up her obsession with vampires and with death.

Whether vampires existed or not, there were worse things. And better things. The baby she carried would be one of those things, a child of the demon which had tried to kill her with orgasms.

She clutched her belly as she leaned over the toilet. She hadn't gotten any bigger yet, but she felt him inside her. She felt what he felt. She felt his power, in her, the same power which had once pulsed through Rick's veins.

ACKNOWLEDGMENTS

Sins of Blood and Stone was first published in 2002 by Catalyst Press. Thank you, Monica, for seeing something here and believing in me.

I wrote the first draft before I knew anyone in the industry, when I thought I would be exclusively a horror author, when I was much younger than I am now, years before it was published.

You can see hints of where I was going, but this is a raw look at where I started.

Special thanks to Gina, who gifted me with a gargoyle who protects me to this day, partly as a going away gift and partly to congratulate me for finishing a manuscript called *The Gargoyle*.

Between writing that and initial publication, I had the help and support of good friends, like the other horsemen (Brian, Mike, Mikey, and Coop).

Since the initial publication, Momo saw to it that I never forgot a follow-up was waiting to be written. It's because of that follow-up that this book is being re-printed today.

As always, a special thanks to Sabine and the Rose Fairy, with me when the book was initially published and with me still.

ABOUT THE AUTHOR

John Urbancik was born in Manhattan in the latter half of the Twentieth Century and started creating his terrible little stories as early as fourth grade.

In addition to books of poetry and a nonfiction book based on his podcast *Inkstains*, Urbancik has written the *DarkWalker* series, *Stale Reality* (also available in Russian), *La Casa del Diablo*, and the collection *The Museum of Curiosities*.

John Urbancik has lived in a great many places, but currently resides at an undisclosed location in the woods of Pennsylvania near the Susquehanna River.

ALSO BY JOHN URBANCIK

NOVELS
Sins of Blood and Stone
Breath of the Moon
Once Upon a Time in Midnight
Stale Reality
The Corpse and the Girl from Miami

DarkWalker 1: Hunting Grounds   DarkWalker 2: Inferno
DarkWalker 3: The Deep City   DarkWalker 4: Armageddon
DarkWalker 5: Ghost Stories   DarkWalker 6: Other Realms

NOVELLAS
A Game of Colors
The Rise and Fall of Babylon (with Brian Keene)
Wings of the Butterfly
House of Shadow and Ash
Necropolis
Quicksilver
Beneath Midnight
Zombies vs. Aliens vs. Robots vs. Cowboys vs.
Ninja vs. Investment Bankers vs. Green Berets
Colette and the Tiger
The Night Carnival
La Casa del Diablo

COLLECTIONS
Shadows, Legends & Secrets
Sound and Vision
Tales of the Fantastic and the Phantasmagoric
The Museum of Curiosities

POETRY
John the Revelator
Odyssey

NONFICTION
InkStained: On Creativity, Writing, and Art

OTHER BOOKS
Multiple volumes of *InkStains*
Choose Your Doom

www.ingramcontent.com/pod-product-compliance
Lightning Source LLC
Chambersburg PA
CBHW052030240626
47153CB00006B/2034